CUT THROAT

A DI FRANK MILLER NOVEL

JOHN CARSON

DI FRANK MILLER SERIES

Crash Point
Silent Marker
Rain Town
Watch Me Bleed
Broken Wheels
Sudden Death
Under the Knife
Trial and Error
Warning Sign
Cut Throat
Blood from a Stone
Time of Death

Frank Miller Crime Series – Books 1-3 – Box set
Frank Miller Crime Series - Books 4-6 - Box set

MAX DOYLE SERIES

SCOTT MARSHALL SERIES

Old Habits

WARNING SIGN

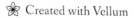 Created with Vellum

For my stepson, Eric

PROLOGUE

'Welcome to summer in Scotland,' Nancy Corbett said, looking up at the dark sky as the snow started falling again.

Stuart Love laughed and squeezed her hand tighter. 'It's not too bad. It's a beautiful place. Besides, it's not summer for another week.'

'I know. I just can't wait to get back home so we can plan our wedding. Sitting on a sandy beach in the Caribbean is a better prospect than tramping through this snow.'

'Have patience, my love. Get it? Because you'll be my *Love*.'

'I get it, Stuart. For the hundredth time.'

He laughed out loud again, his voice infectious.

The snow had been falling all day and it made the

town of Langholm look like it should be on a Christmas card.

They walked hand-in-hand from the Abernethy Theatre, their boots crunching through the snow on the pavement.

Love seemed to have a smile fixed permanently on his face. 'This is a dream come true for me,' he said. He knew he'd told her this many times but he imagined it was the same when you checked your lottery ticket and found you had six numbers.

'Your mum and dad would have been proud,' Nancy said.

'I know they would. But at least my aunts are proud.'

'That's something anyway. They were so happy when you got the role on that hospital drama. You were a household name overnight.'

They had reached the corner and stopped before the road bridge that spanned the River Esk.

'Give me a kiss,' Stuart said, laughing again.

Nancy slapped his arm. 'I will not. What if somebody sees us? I'm here with you, you're going to put on the Hugh Abernethy play and we're going to have our faces splashed in the papers, and then we're going to start our new life in Hollywood.'

'In that order.'

'But first, I think we deserve a little drink in the hotel before heading up to our room,' said Nancy.

'I agree.'

The river ran dark alongside them as they walked along the road which had been roughly ploughed. At the end was the footbridge that crossed the Esk, and one of the churches faced them.

'Let's go in the playground!' Nancy said.

'Oh, Nance, come on, I'm tired,' said Stuart.

'You weren't tired a minute ago when I said we should have a drink before heading off to bed. Are you trying to tell me I'm with an old man who can only manage it once a week?'

'Okay, so long as I don't have to take my boots off!'

She laughed and ran into the churchyard, then through the wall into the playground. The snow was coming down harder as Stuart followed.

He heard her squeals as she started swinging. Then she started screaming.

'Christ, Nance, it's only a swing,' he said as he walked through the gap in the church wall.

The swing was moving to and fro, but it was empty.

'Nancy!' he shouted. There was no reply. The snow was falling heavier now, the air bone-chilling. Stuart walked forward, looking at the ground. Foot-steps were in the snow, heading away from the playground. Just one set. He followed them to the wall that surrounded the playground.

Another gap was set in the high wall that separated the playground from the graveyard beyond.

The footsteps went through. Stuart followed.

He didn't have to go far. The gravestones were topped with snow. The ground looked like a white blanket had been thrown over it.

'Nancy?' he said, feeling the shiver run down his spine.

But Nancy didn't reply.

She was standing staring at the dead woman. At the nails that had been driven through her hands, each one pinned to a separate tree, a few feet apart.

Stuart walked past his girlfriend and looked at the woman.

Her throat had been cut.

He was the one who was screaming now.

ONE

'I have some news,' Lou Purcell said to his son as he stamped his feet on the doormat. The apartment building had doormats at the entrance, but his son Percy, made him take his boots off anyway.

'I hope your feet are not bogging,' Percy said, making a face as his father took the boots off.

'I'm sure the stench of yours will overcome anything wafting off mine. Now, you got the coffee on?'

'It's a weekday morning and I have work, so that would be a yes.' Percy shut the door after Lou dropped his footwear on an indoor mat.

'What is this news?' They went into the living room. Suzy, Percy's wife, was pouring a coffee when he came in.

'Thanks, Suzy,' Lou said, sitting down at the table.

'Come on, don't keep me in suspense. How much have you won?'

'What?'

'I can't believe you would come round here at this time of the morning without the news I've been waiting years to hear; you won the lottery,' said Percy.

'Not exactly.'

'Well, bog off back to your own gaff instead of coming round here and scranning my bacon.'

'Percy!' Suzy said. 'Can I get you a bacon roll, Lou?'

'That would be smashing, love.'

'Don't encourage him, Suzy. You're not here to run about after him.'

'*You* can make me one then,' said Lou.

'Yeah, and while I'm at it, I'll polish your boots for you.'

'I don't mind making a bacon roll for my favourite father-in-law,' Suzy said.

'This isn't a Victorian novel where the wife scoots into the kitchen to wait on the menfolk,' Percy said to Lou. 'Mind and put some ketchup on mine. Thanks.'

Lou shook his head. 'Sexist wee sod.'

'We take turns each morning if you must know. But stop dodging the point; what news do you have? And I hope it's no such nonsense like at Christmas when you found out you were born into a family of gypsies.'

'You'd love that, eh? Having a family that stuck by each other and looked out for one another,' said Lou.

'Just get on with it.'

'Right; me and Bruce have found a place.'

'Well, I hope you'll both be very happy together. Am I getting an invite to the wedding?'

Lou shook his head. 'It's a sad day when a father can't have a serious conversation with his son.'

'Nothing wrong with being gay.'

'Jesus. I am not gay, and even if I was, it's normal nowadays.'

'That's what I just said. Have you turned deaf as well?'

'But to clarify, Mr Smartarse, we got an office,' said Lou.

'And where is this place?'

'Down a close.'

'Has Sam Spade picked a business name for himself yet?'

'He was one of you lot, remember?' said Lou. 'Why can't you be a bit more serious?'

Suzy came through with the rolls and sat down at the table. 'I worry about you, Lou. I don't want you getting into anything dangerous. Percy doesn't want you to either.'

'I know. He's made himself clear many times.'

'You're in your sixties, and you're going around like you're James Bond,' Percy said.

'Here we go again. I've told you before, I'll be doing some of the grunt work. Surveillance and that sort of thing. I won't be jumping out of airplanes or scaling the side of a building. Just the boring stuff. Something that doesn't take a lot of brain power. Like your job.'

'As long as you know what you're getting yourself into. No buying stun guns off shady websites.'

'I won't need to. I bought an illegal handgun.'

Percy and Suzy looked at him as he took a bite of his roll.

'I'm kidding.'

'Good,' Percy said.

'It's a shotgun.'

'You've been watching too many reruns of The Bill.'

'Okay. I bought an extendable baton. Although technically, it's a device for breaking the window in a car if you're trapped.'

'For God's sake, you'll get arrested for belting somebody with a deadly weapon.'

'No I won't. Bloody worrywart.'

'Just so we're straight, I won't be bailing you out. You'll be fighting for the soap-on-a-rope in the showers in Saughton all on your own.'

'Bruce is keeping me right, don't worry.' Bruce

Hagan was an ex-detective who had befriended Lou after the old man had asked him for some help.

'As long as he's paying you.'

'He will, once the jobs come in. Right now, he's teaching me to play chess.'

'It's not as glamourous as you might think.'

'I dunno. Chess is okay,' said Lou, smiling.

'Fine. Don't take me seriously. Find out the hard way.'

'I don't think Bruce ordered a Ferrari for me to drive around in. It will be cheating husbands we're following or something like that. Missing persons. You know, the jobs that you lot are supposed to do.' He looked at Suzy. 'No offence.'

'None taken, Lou.' She patted his hand.

'Anyway, I just wanted to keep you in the loop.'

'You mean, you wanted to give me a heads-up that you'll be bugging me at the station when you get stuck on a case?'

'That laddie's bright. Although not bright enough, or else he would have had my coffee mug filled again by now.'

TWO

'Christ, did you have a stroke or something, Miller?' DCI Paddy Gibb said from the back seat of the car as he sat up straight again.

'I thought you had dozed off,' DS Andy Watt said from the front seat.

'You're a pair of bloody comedians.' Gibb looked at Miller. 'You might want to give me a heads-up next time you want to play at being a bloody rally driver. And this is not your Audi you're driving. Christ, I thought I was a goner.'

DI Frank Miller looked at the boss. 'Technically, sir, according to Section 8, sub-section 41, paragraph 9 of the Police Handbook, when a senior officer is riding in the back of a police vehicle, the officer is required to be wearing a seatbelt.'

'Stop talking pish, Miller.'

'Okay.'

'I've got mine on,' Watt said, pulling the belt out in front of him. 'I'm a good officer though.'

'Shut your piehole. And I was not sleeping, I was merely observing the location – before I got thrown about.' He looked out of the window. 'Where the hell are we anyway?'

'Hawick. The main road into town.' The Vauxhall was sideways across the entrance to a small side street.

The snow was coming down harder. Miller looked out of the rear window and saw the other Vauxhall with the two female officers in it, DS Julie Stott and DS Steffi Walker. Gibb looked round at the car, too.

'See? They don't have their car upside down. Next time remind me to wear my brown trousers when you're driving.'

'I brought it to a controlled stop,' Miller said, as a voice came through on their radio.

'Controlled my arse. You nearly had us through a fucking hedge.'

'You alright in front?' Steffi Walker.

The men looked at each other. 'You couldn't have lost control round the corner where they couldn't see us, no? Now we'll never hear the end of it.'

'I didn't plan on the car going arse sideways.' The wheels spun a bit before gripping again.

'When I say you made a James Hunt of going

round that corner, I'm not paying homage to the late racing driver.' The DCI looked out of the back window at the other car. 'That lassie took the corner like she's been driving in this stuff all her life.'

'That's a bit sexist, is it not, boss?' Watt said. 'Against us, I mean.'

'Just an observation, son.'

'First pint tonight's on you, boss, and I might just manage to keep that out of my report.'

'If I read any shite about me being sexist, you'll be transferred down here permanently.'

'I wouldn't mind that. God's own country, this is,' Miller said.

'Well, you can bloody well join him, then.'

Miller laughed and got the car going on the main road again.

'Why are you all grumpy-drawers this morning?' Watt said. 'Missing Maggie already?'

'Give it a rest. We're two colleagues who go out for a drink now and again,' said Gibb.

'You better start drinking Red Bull at your age.'

'Andy, I swear to Christ, I will make you disappear down in this place if you don't shut up.'

'I'm just saying. Look at young Frank there; got a three-month-old baby now, probably taking care of Kim twice a week.'

'Three times a week,' Miller said.

'Three times a week. He's young and fit. You, on the other hand...'

'Am about to go to prison for killing a detective sergeant.'

'He's just looking out for you, boss,' Miller said.

'Don't encourage him.' Gibb took out his packet of cigarettes. *Which one of you little bastards is going to die first?* He popped one out and lit it.

'And there we have it,' Watt said. 'Grumpy-breeks was needing a nicotine fix.'

'What does the handbook say about a senior officer smoking in the pool car then, Miller?'

'It says that any officer of DCI rank and above can smoke whenever he bloody well feels like. As long as he rolls the window down even when it's chucking down snow outside.'

Gibb rolled the window down. 'If you pair of bastards smoked, I wouldn't have to roll the window down.'

'Roll it back up again, Paddy, I'm freezing my nuts off here,' Watt complained.

'Ever had a haircut with a lighter before?' Gibb flicked his lighter a couple of times behind Watt's head before rolling the window back up. 'Christ, I think I would rather let you two reprobates suck in second-hand smoke than lose the feeling in my face.'

Watt started coughing, exaggerating it.

'Carry on, Watt, and I'll chain-smoke the rest of the way there.'

The rest of the way there was uneventful. Miller kept the car on the road for the next twenty miles as they entered Langholm in one piece. They couldn't see the monument on the hill for the snow. The sky was full of it.

Watt turned round to Gibb. 'Did Jeni Bridge say we were to get a tab at the bar since we'll be stuck here indefinitely?'

'No, she bloody well didn't. Besides, I won't need a tab. You'll be paying mine.'

'Oh dear, old Grumpy-boots is going to be sorely disappointed,' Watt said to Miller.

They drove down past the Kilngreen, a park area in front of the river. In the summer, a fair was here for the Langholm Common Riding, but now it was like everything else, covered in snow.

'We'll get settled into our digs then go and see the sergeant who was called out to the scene,' Gibb said.

'I hope Haggis McPorridge is on the ball,' Watt said.

'I'm sure they've got it sussed, Andy,' said Miller, slowing down at the Thomas Telford bridge. 'Is it just me or is this snow getting heavier?'

'The land beyond doom,' Gibb said. 'You couldn't pay me enough to live in a small town.'

'The Muckle Toon, they call it,' Watt said. 'What does that mean?'

Neither Gibb nor Miller had the answer.

They rounded the corner and were in the high street. They were still on the A7, a main arterial road that ran through the Borders to Carlisle in the north of England.

Watt pointed out of the window. 'Look, a Bank of Scotland and a Royal Bank on the other side. The Royal has an ATM, Frank, so you won't have an excuse not to put your hand in your pocket at the bar.'

'You're the only man I know who has a fishing line tied to a tenner, Andy.'

'My reputation precedes me.'

The Crown Hotel was on their left. The roads were getting slicker. An articulated truck was coming towards them. 'This town should have a bypass by now,' Miller said, saying a silent prayer that the driver hadn't fallen asleep at the wheel. 'Where's our hotel?'

'The Eskdale. It's there on the right, on the corner, but the car park is in a little square round the back. It's a one-way, apparently. Go past the town hall, which is also the police station, and turn left,' Gibb said.

Miller made it round. The library was the back half of the town hall building. He pulled into Parliament Square, the road now covered with snow. The women followed suit and parked beside them.

'The town hall is also the police station?'

'I'm glad that your hearing is still okay,' Gibb said. 'They used to have their own station but it got closed down years ago. Now they share the town hall, and the library is in the back of the building.'

They all got out. Miller looked at the sky but it was thick with snow and dropping it hard.

'That wasn't so bad,' Julie Stott said as they got out of their own car. 'You managed to recover the car well, sir,' she said to Miller, and she and Steffi Walker smiled. Miller could feel his cheeks going red.

'The only reason you two didn't skid is because you saw where he skidded and avoided it,' Watt said.

'Yeah, that's it, Andy.' Julie opened the doors and they took their holdalls. The cars locked, they made their way across the main road to the hotel.

It was a typical country hotel, full of old charm and warmth. The bar looked promising.

They approached the desk to check-in.

'I'm afraid there's been a mistake,' the woman said. 'You appear to have been double-booked.'

'How can that be?' Gibb said.

'We have the literary festival happening this week. We had most of our rooms booked. There are only two rooms left. One with a single, and one with a double.'

'I'll have the double,' Gibb said. 'Fight amongst yourselves. One room going spare.'

16

The others looked at each other. 'Julie, you have the room. We'll find something else,' Steffi said.

'That's good of you. I'll buy you a drink tonight.'

'Like my rooms, I like a double,' said Steffi.

Gibb looked at the woman. 'Would you know the number of the other hotels for my other three officers?'

'They're all fully booked. We keep in touch with each other. There's a rooming house at the other end of the High Street. I can call there and see if there's anything.'

'Please.'

'Fuck's sake, a rooming house. One step up from a borstal,' Watt said to Miller in a whisper.

Julie took her key and headed upstairs. 'We'll see you shortly.'

'None of your bloody shenanigans while we're here,' Gibb said to Miller and Watt as Julie went up the stairs and out of earshot.

'I'm in a relationship and Frank's married, if you don't mind,' Watt said. 'May I remind you that you're the only one who isn't attached. Apart from your weekend girlfriend. And the one you blow up when you're feeling a bit frisky.'

'Don't talk pish. Just keep this professional.'

'Again, we're here to work. Me and the good inspector here don't want to get a call in the middle of the night saying Wee Willie Winkie's creeping about the hotel.'

'Shut up.'

The woman put her hand over the mouthpiece. 'They have the last three rooms available. Shall I tell her to reserve them?'

'Please.' *Thank you, God.* Gibb grinned at Miller and Watt. 'Get along there. Get your stuff unpacked and get back to the station across the road. I'm going to call the station and get that sergeant to make sure we have a Land Rover to get about in.'

'How far along is it?' Miller asked.

'About five minutes' walk. It's right next to the Bank of Scotland.'

The three detectives picked up their bags and went out into the cold, the snow driving harder.

'I'm assuming a boarding house doesn't have a bar,' Watt said, pulling up his collar with one hand.

'Or a minibar. I could do with a wee nip right now. Maybe later tonight we could come back to the hotel, Andy, and Gibb will feel bad where we got landed and he'll force feed us whisky.'

'I wouldn't count on it, Frank.'

'Don't worry, boys, I'll buy you a drink,' Steffi said, 'if you let me hold on to one of you.'

'Here, take my arm, Steffi,' Watt said. 'Frank's not much of a drinker.'

They trudged along the pavement, past a little newsagent and some other shops until they came to the bank. Miller rang the bell at the door next to it.

An older woman answered. 'Yes?'

'I'm DI Miller, this is DS Watt, DS Walker. We're the guests you're expecting.'

She looked them up and down like there was a bad smell lingering before stepping back and opening the door.

'Wipe your feet,' she ordered.

'On the way out,' Watt said under his breath. The detectives stomped on her doormat before they were shown into the house. A little bar was tucked under the stairs, and Watt actually got his hopes up before realising this was the reception area.

'I'll need a copy of your credit cards,' she said.

'We're Police Scotland, not a bunch of scallys,' Watt said.

Miller produced his docket and Watt handed his over. 'These should suffice. The police are picking up the tab.'

'Must be nice.'

'No, The Ritz would be nice,' Watt said.

The woman looked at him. 'You're welcome to try and find something else.'

'This is fine,' Miller said. 'Thank you.'

The woman signed them in and handed them each

a key. 'Upstairs and round to the left, for you two,' she said to Miller and Steffi. 'Both rooms face the high street. And you can have the last room at the back,' she said to Watt.

They took their keys without further comment.

'My name's Elizabeth, but you may call me Bunty. All my regulars do. We have other visitors like yourselves, of course. Dinner is served at six pm sharp. If you're not in by six fifteen, don't bother.'

She left them and they climbed the stairs in what was once a large, terraced house.

'There's a Chinese takeaway across the road, and a small hotel with a public bar that serves meals,' Watt said.

'I saw. That's good back-up.'

They reached a landing. Two smaller staircases split off, one to the front and one to the back.

'I hope Gibb's room has a draft,' Watt said. 'He gets the four poster and we get Cunty Bunty. The sheets better be fucking fresh, that's all I'm saying. It better not be one of those places that are so bad, the bedbugs have moved out.' He stomped off and Miller and Steffi went up the flight to the front of the house.

'See you downstairs,' Miller said to her.

Miller's room was neat and tidy. It had a double bed, a TV, and a unique country-air smell. He took his phone out and dialled his wife, Kim.

'Thank God you got there in one piece,' she said.

'We're fine but the snow is getting heavier by the minute.'

'Did you have the radio on in the car?'

'No. We were fighting over what station to listen to so we kept it off.'

'You're like a bunch of wee boys.' She laughed. 'But seriously, they keep updating the news about the Beast from the East number two. It's going to be far worse than the first one. Wind and snow coming from Siberia again, but it's supposed to be much heavier.'

'Paddy's going to get us one of the Land Rover's from the locals.'

'Stay safe, Frank, and call me every day.'

'I will. How are my two little ladies?'

'Emma says she will take care of Charlie while you're away, and Annie misses you. I know she's only three months old but I can see it in her eyes.'

'And what about my big girl? Does Miss Kim miss her hubby?'

'Of course, I do, Miller.'

'God knows how long we'll be down here.'

'I have my folks here, so we'll be fine. And my friends. And Jack and Samantha just along the landing.'

'The only thing missing is me.'

'Absence makes the heart grow fonder. We'll find

out if it's true. But seeing as you're with two single females…'

'Don't even think about finishing that sentence, lady.'

Kim laughed. 'Just kidding. I trust you.'

'Like you won't be having any parties while I'm away.'

'With two young kids? Give me a break.'

'With that storm coming, I hope you don't go stir crazy.'

'Oh, I'll be out and about, don't worry. If I have to leave the little one, it will be with your dad and Sam, just so I can get some groceries.'

'Right, I'll get going. Paddy wants us back along at the station so we can meet the local crew.'

'Okay, honey. Call me whenever you can.'

'I will.'

He disconnected the call and looked out of the window down into the high street. The snow wasn't letting up, but they had more to worry about.

A dead woman who had been murdered needed their help in finding her killer.

THREE

Haggis McPorridge turned out to be Dan *Chubby* Brown, but at six foot five, not many people called him *Chubby* to his face.

'He's a big bastard,' Gibb said as Miller, Watt and Steffi walked into the Thomas Hope Hospital. He'd called them to say to come here instead of the station.

Watt and Miller took their woollen hats off and stamped their feet on the mat just inside the front door.

'You lot didn't have to come far, but we did,' Watt said to Gibb and Julie. 'You could have sent the Land Rover along to get us.'

'Next time I'll call Uber, or maybe get the police helicopter to pick you up. But I think you need the exercise, son.'

Watt looked down at his gut. 'What does he mean by that?'

The small hospital was just round from the hotel, a minute's walk. Gibb shook his head. 'Always complaining. Never mind that, Sergeant Brown is through with one of the doctors.'

Julie Stott came through a door. 'They're ready for us whenever you're ready, sir.'

'We're coming, sergeant.'

They followed her through to a laboratory suite and a cold storage facility.

'This is a small hospital, so this isn't where they do post-mortems, but the mortuary is where they store the deceased until the undertaker takes them away, either to the funeral director's premises, or the mortuary in Dumfries for post-mortem,' Julie said.

They went into the mortuary where the doctor and two uniformed officers were standing. Julie Stott joined Steffi Walker and they stood off to one side.

'This is getting to be quite the party,' Dr Eve Ross said. Miller looked at the woman; she appeared to be in her mid-forties, short in stature but big in presence. The sergeant was indeed a big man, not chubby at all, but built like he didn't just play on a rugby team but *was* the rugby team. The other uniform was a young man, maybe early twenties.

'This is the rest of my team,' Gibb said, introducing Miller and Watt.

'How many more officers are based here?' Miller asked Brown.

'There are ten of us. I'm in charge, and there are nine other officers.'

'Brown and I discussed setting up an incident room along at the station,' Gibb said.

'We have six fridges here, which is a bit of an overkill, but that's how it was built,' Dr Ross said. 'There's never any more than two used at one time. For deceased, anyway. We use one of the others to keep our milk and sandwiches cold.' She looked at the faces. Only Brown was smiling. 'I'm kidding, of course. We do have a fridge through in the canteen.'

'Get on with it, for fuck's sake,' Watt whispered to Miller.

'You say something, sergeant?' Brown said.

'If I did, *sergeant*, you'd be the first to know.'

'Let's get her out,' Gibb said.

One of the lab's techs opened up a fridge at chest level and pulled out the sliding tray. The woman was covered by a white sheet. It was pulled back to reveal a woman whose skin was pale and her throat had been slashed. She hadn't been cleaned but left the way she was found. Dried blood was on her neck and chest. The palm of each hand had a puncture wound.

'You took photos of the scene?' Gibb said.

'This isn't our first one. It's not like the big, bad

city, but we've had a murder here before,' Brown said, turning towards the other uniform. 'Remember that fairground worker, Jones? Got into a fight with a gypsy...'

'Maybe we could compare tales from the big, bad city and your little town later, sergeant,' Gibb said, ignoring the look Brown gave him. Miller suspected that not many men interrupted Brown.

'Yes, we took photos. We even sent them to Edinburgh. We don't have sawdust between our ears.'

'And yet, here we are,' Watt said, 'the professionals.'

'Step outside,' Gibb said to Sergeant Brown, and Miller figured that wasn't a line Brown heard much in a pub.

Brown followed Gibb into the corridor and Gibb waited until the door had closed behind them.

'You listen to me, son; I don't give a shit how big you are. I've dealt with harder schoolboys who were bigger than you. I've dealt with all sorts of shite in Edinburgh. That's why I'm Chief Inspector Gibb, and you're Sergeant Brown. I don't give a rat's arse how you speak to other people you come across, but you will not, and I repeat, *will not* speak to my team in any way you fancy. We're here for a murder investigation and if you don't like us encroaching on your territory, then tough shit. I can make one phone call and have your arse over to Dumfries in a heartbeat. Do I make myself clear on that, sergeant?'

Brown managed to look sheepish. 'Yes, sir. I apologise. It won't happen again.'

'Good. See it doesn't.'

They went back inside, Gibb wanting to pull out his cigarettes, but he thought he might be tempted to stub one out on Jones's eyeball, the way the young man was grinning.

'Pay attention, Jones!' Brown said, wiping the smirk off the younger man's face with his words.

'Okay, boys, now that we've sorted out who can piss up a wall the furthest, can we get down to business?' It was a rhetorical question. 'I'm not a pathologist, but unless the woman died of heart failure, I would hazard a guess that the gash in her throat was the cause of her demise. A cut like that would mean she wouldn't be alive for longer than a couple of minutes afterwards. The sharp object cut through her carotid.'

Gibb looked at Brown. 'I want every background detail you have on this woman. Has her identity been confirmed?'

'Yes, sir,' Jones said. 'Ella Fitzroy aged fifty-five, formally identified by her sister, Ann, who lives in the town here.'

'We covered her so only her face was showing,' Dr Ross said.

'Good,' said Gibb. When is she being picked up for transportation to Dumfries?'

'Depends on the weather. We were waiting for you and your team to arrive, so you could see her.'

'That's fine. We'll regroup at the station. Sergeant, when you're ready.'

The officers trooped out of the hospital into the blinding snow and walked across the road to the station.

'I think Oor Wullie took the huff,' Watt said as they got inside.

'He's a big bairn. They're used to doing things differently down here.' Gibb shook the snow off his head.

'As long as we get the job done and nobody gets in our way,' Miller said,

'How's your hotel?' asked Julie as they walked.

'Oh, that's it, rub it in. The boarding house looks like something out of an Alfred Hitchcock film. All we need now is a load of birds tapping at the windows and to find out the old closet who runs the place is really a bloke and that will be the icing on the cake.'

'At least we have our own rooms, Andy,' Watt said.

'You boys not sharing, then?' Julie, said as they entered the warmth.

28

'No, the honeymoon suite was taken, so we're stuck with our own private rooms. We have to share the lavvy that we have to navigate to in the middle of the night. Up and downstairs. That's going to be barry when we're pished.'

'You're not here on a bloody stag do, Watt,' Gibb reminded him.

'This is a small Borders town. What else do you think they do down here for fun? It's not socialising down here, it's a way of life. They start drinking when they're twelve.'

There was another sergeant behind the public counter. 'You'll be the city slickers,' he said.

'What's your name?'

'Sergeant Hudson.'

'I'm DCI Gibb, son. You can call me sir. Same with DI Miller there. If you want to be a smartarse and start showing disrespect, I can call my boss right now and have you transferred somewhere far away. And if you think I'm joking, son, just you keep on pulling my fucking chain. Now, show us in so we can get the ball rolling.'

'Yes, sir. Sorry, sir.'

'Why are they all a bunch of smartarses down here?' Gibb said, not too quietly.

'They're not used to police work. It's all looking for

missing sheep and seeing old women across the road,' Watt said.

The surly sergeant showed the team upstairs to a room, which could be a training room or a make-shift canteen, depending on whether or not there were empty sandwich packets lying around.

They hung their jackets up. 'I'd like whatever officers there are on duty to be here. Those who aren't can be filled in later,' Gibb said.

Brown and Jones came in, followed by two other officers, one of them a female.

'Right, son, you can start with the crime scene photos. And somebody get us a coffee.'

Brown nudged Jones, who left the room to find a kettle.

'Let me introduce us,' Gibb said, and then they all heard the massive boom.

FOUR

The Beast was coming and Ewan for one didn't want to get stuck before it bit. The big Scania hauling the petrol tanker was a good truck, but the laws of physics applied to everything, even the truck.

Ewan had been driving for ten years almost, and he'd never seen such bad weather or heavy snow. It was blinding at times, and sometimes he could hardly see the road.

He wanted to get through Langholm and make it to Carlisle if he could. He just had to get through this damn town, with its narrow streets and arseholes who didn't know how to slow down for a fucking truck.

'Jesus Christ!' he said, slamming on the brakes. He hadn't noticed the van coming out of the farm track near the bridge.

The traffic lights had been added years before, because of bad drivers, and they were green. He had been watching them, focusing intently on them, hoping to God they would stay green so he could downshift and navigate over the narrow bridge.

The van didn't even have any fucking lights on. Ewan leant on the horn but the van drove slowly in front of him. Still a green light, but now he was concentrating on not going right up the arse of this stupid bugger.

The snow was coming down like wet, heavy feathers, covering everything and sticking. It was blinding, the wipers fighting a losing battle.

Ewan saw it wasn't a van but a commercial Land Rover, painted white. He had no lights on. What in the name of Christ was this stupid bastard doing? Slowing right down on a green light with a truck up his arse.

Ewan leaned on the horn. The Land Rover stopped. God Almighty. Ewan stood on the brakes like his life depended on it. The truck came to a juddering halt, and his heart was hammering in his chest.

He put the handbrake on and took the truck out of gear, leaving it to idle. He opened the door and jumped down. He didn't care if this was a farmer who lived round here. Ewan was always up for a go with some stupid bastard who drove like a prick. The roads were full of them.

He pulled up his collar against the driving snow. The smug sheep-shagger was still sitting in the car. The exhaust was blowing in the wind. Maybe Ewan should suggest the guy go home and sit doing that in his garage with the door closed.

'Right, you stupid bast—' he started to say as the car's door was opened and the man with the ski mask stepped out. He had something in his hand. Ewan quickly turned round to see if there were any other drivers behind him who could see what was going on, but the road was empty.

He turned back to Ski Mask. Shit, there was another one running across the narrow bridge on foot. The driver of the Land Rover turned to look at his friend for a moment.

'Look, pal, no harm, no foul, eh?' Ewan said.

Ski Mask number one turned back to him and jabbed him with the Taser. Ewan felt like a thousand horses had just kicked him all at once.

'Take the Land Rover to the wall,' Eddie Hooper said. Ken Smart nodded and jumped behind the wheel of the big car and drove it on to the bridge. Nothing was coming the other way, because Smart had put out a sign that said, *Road Closed Ahead*, just beyond the house that sat on its own further back. He had played around with the traffic-light control box on the other side of the bridge.

The whiteout conditions meant there was very little on the roads and what there was wouldn't see anything on the approach to the road closed sign, but nothing appeared.

Hooper brought out a set of cable ties and got Ewan's hands behind his back and put the ties on. They lifted him into the back of their Land Rover. Smart drove it across the bridge to the other side. Hooper got in behind the wheel of the truck, shut the door, and drove the big Scania forward until it was closing in on the stone wall of the bridge then he floored the accelerator then jumped out, rolling on the snow-covered ground.

The Scania smashed through the side of the bridge before coming to a halt, hanging precariously. Hooper walked round the back of the large vehicle and squeezed past. He had made sure there was enough room for him to get by so he wasn't stuck on the opposite side of the river.

Two petrol cans were lying in the road. They grabbed one each, Hooper dousing the cab while Smart doused the wires and connections at the fifth wheel, making sure the liquid was going underneath. Then he went round to the side and opened one of the taps.

As the petrol was starting to pour out, Hooper lit a Molotov cocktail and threw it into the cab, followed by one at the tanker and they ran as fast as they could through the snow to their other Land Rover. They took off at speed as the flames caught hold of the truck.

The flames grew more violent but the men were well away when the tanker blew.

FIVE

'What was that?' Gibb asked.

The first boom was followed by another. 'Explosions close by,' Miller said.

Sergeant Hudson darted away while the others were gathered round the whiteboard that was displaying a photo of the killer's victim.

'There's been an accident up at the bridge, on the north side of town,' the sergeant said, coming back into the room. 'A petrol tanker's crashed and exploded.'

'Do you need our help?' Gibb asked.

'No, we farmers down here have dealt with traffic accidents before, thank you, Chief Inspector.' He gave Gibb a look as the others left the station. But then the sergeant stopped and looked at Gibb again. 'Jones can stay here and fill you in.'

And with that, they were gone.

'Right, constable, I want you to go through every-thing from last night,' Miller said. 'And did you find the kettle?'

'I did, sir.'

Gibb looked at the young man. 'Go and get the coffee going, son, and then tell us in your own words what went on last night.'

Sometimes PC Nick Jones thought he lived in the land that time forgot. He wanted to be a big city detective, heading up to Edinburgh. Christ, what a city that was. They had a bowling alley and everything. Want to go ice skating? Check. Movies, dancing? Check and hell yeah! He had spoken to his friend about moving up there, and his pal had said he fancied it too. They could get a flat together, share the rent and the likes, but his friend was a bit of a lazy bastard.

PC Gilbert Morris had ambitions too, but Nick thought it might take his friend a little bit longer to get things going. Sometimes, he had to light a fire under his mate just to do anything.

The station was closed at night. There were still three of them on duty, but every night was like the zombie apocalypse had happened, unless it was a Friday or Saturday night, when a few of the locals had to be helped out of a pub or hotel. There was never any real fighting, just people having one too many.

Then the call had come in that would change everything.

'We've had a report of a dead woman in the graveyard behind the church,' Sergeant Brown had said. 'Go and check it out.'

Nick and Gibby had stood up from their desks and Nick had grabbed the keys for one of the Land Rovers.

'Better than sitting in there listening to Chubby farting all night,' Nick said, tossing the keys to Gibby.

'Smelly bastard. And we can't even open a window, it's so cold.'

They'd got in the big SUV and fired it up. 'Lights and sirens?' Gibby asked.

'Nah, fuck it. Probably some old boot saw a squirrel or something. Got scared and called 999.'

'Aye, probably pished an' all.' He backed the car out and the beam from the headlights bounced off the drifting snow.

'It's gonna be a fucking belter, this storm,' Gibby said, driving along to the Thomas Telford bridge, named after the famous engineer who was born in the town.

'You give any more thought to transferring up to Edinburgh with me?' Nick asked.

'I have actually. I think that would be a great idea. Me and you in CID or something.'

'Aye, Brown can stick his station up his arse. I'm going to get on with it once this storm is over.'

'What about Alison?'

'What about her? There are plenty of *Alisons* up in Edinburgh.'

'Her father will kill you if he thinks you've been leading his daughter on.'

'Let's not tell him then. We'll wait until the transfer's been approved and then we'll say we've been seconded and we have to go at short notice.'

'Aye, seconded. Great idea. Then we can still dally with the ladies and they won't be any the wiser. Or else they might get some idea about coming up with us.'

'Aye, fuck that for a game of soldiers. Left in there, ya dozy bastard,' he said pointing to the entrance to the churchyard.

Gibby hauled on the steering wheel and for a second, Nick thought they were going to go crashing through the pedestrian bridge next to the church entrance, but Gibby brought the vehicle under control.

'Fuck me, pay attention, I nearly shat myself there.'

The windscreen wipers batted the snow away as they drove over the darkened bridge. 'Fucking hell, this place is scary.'

'It's a lot lighter because of the snow,' Nick said, wishing the Landie would heat up soon.

'Still, there's nobody around here.'

'You're a copper, you're not supposed to be scared of the dark,' Nick said, laughing out loud. 'Big fanny.'

'Fuck off. My gran died not so long ago, remember? What if it's her, come back from the dead? Maybe she can't stand being in the ground and wants her family back.'

'Away and don't talk shite. Drive round to the back gate.'

The headlights of the SUV picked out the black gates that were opened when there was a funeral, allowing the hearse and other vehicles through. Nick jumped out and ran over to it, slipping on his way but not falling. He opened the gates and the Land Rover pulled up. He got back in and Gibby drove through, the light bouncing around, illuminating the gravestones.

'Where's that fucking minister when you need him? He should have been out here with a bastard torch leading the way. Probably in his manse watching swimwear TV, having a chug—'

'There!' Gibby screamed, slamming on the brakes and pointing.

'Mother of Christ, will you no' do that! I swear you're trying to give me a fucking heart attack.' They sat and stared out through the windscreen, past the falling snowflakes. Had coloured lights been put on one of the trees, it might have looked like Christmas.

Instead, they saw a macabre scene playing out before them.

The corpse of the woman was standing up between two trees, each hand nailed to a tree. Despite the snow covering her head, they could see the blood that had run down from her neck to cover the front of her coat. Her head was flopped forward, so they couldn't see who it was.

'Call it in,' Nick said in a whisper.

Gibby sat staring.

'Call it in for fuck's sake!' Nick shouted.

'Who turned up?' Gibb asked.

'Sergeant Brown. Then Doctor Ross. The sergeant took photos then the funeral director was called out. He took the body to the hospital, where she was kept overnight until you lot turned up.'

Gibb opened a folder that had been sitting on the table. There were several 8 x 10 colour photos of the scene.

'The snow was falling, you said?' Miller asked the constable.

'Yes, sir. Quite heavy. There was no let-up.'

'Footprints?' Julie said.

Nick turned towards her. 'If there were, they were covered by the time we got there.'

'Who found her?' Gibb said, putting the photos down.

'Two people. Actors from the festival. Stuart Love and his girlfriend, Nancy Corbett. They had been walking back from the theatre and decided to cross the footbridge, but then he—'

Gibb held up a hand. 'I want to hear it from the horse's mouth, so to speak. Where can we find them?'

'They're renting the big mansion up on the hill. They've been here for a week but they seem to spend most of their time in the hotel bar. The same hotel as you. Or along at the theatre.'

'Who took the statements?'

'Sergeant Hudson.'

'What about the victim's family? Apart from her sister?'

'None. She lives with her sister, here in town and they have each other. Both are spinsters.'

Gibb turned towards his team. 'I'll go with the ladies to talk with the actors. You and Watt go and talk to the sister,' he said to Miller, 'then talk to the minister whose graveyard she was found in.'

'What will I do, sir?' Nick asked.

'Go with DI Miller. Show him around. Then we can all compare notes after dinner since the day is getting away from us.'

'Sounds good to me,' Watt said. 'Comparing notes in the bar. You can join us after your shift, son, just to give us the skinny on the place. I'll even let you buy us a pint.'

'Oh, okay,' Nick said.

'There's one born every minute,' Watt whispered as they left the station.

SIX

'What do you do for fun around here, son?' Watt said as the young constable drove the Land Rover away from the station, heading north on the A7.

'Fun? I don't think I've ever had fun since I was posted here.' The four-wheel-drive vehicle's tyres bit into the thick snow on the road.

'That traffic accident must be the sort of thing that keeps you busy, eh?' Miller said.

'Yes, sir. That and inspecting licensed premises, visiting farms to see that they have the right licenses, that sort of thing.' He turned left over the Thomas Telford bridge and headed straight up the road. 'That used to be the old station,' he said, pointing to a red brick building on the corner. There was scaffolding with netting on it covering the front of the old building. A security van sat outside.

He turned left.

'Who owns it now?'

'A developer has it. I don't know what for.' He looked in the mirror at Miller sitting in the back of the car. 'I know I should take more interest in the town, but me and my pal just go drinking on our day off. I couldn't care less about the place. I know that sounds shite, but it's the truth. Everybody under the age of forty wants to escape to the big city. Or *any* big city. Somewhere there's a bit of life.'

'It must be hard living in a small town. I couldn't do it.'

'Aye, it's different when you're born here, you get used to it, but nowadays we have the internet and the young people can see what's out there.'

'That was a bit like Edinburgh centuries ago,' Watt said, 'when there were walls around the city. That's where *The World's End* pub got its name from. For some people, that was literally the end of the world.'

The tyres crunched through the snow as it was slowly building up on the road. It was still coming down heavy, the wipers swiping it away. Nick slowed the big vehicle down. 'That's true of this town; the end of the world. That's why me and my mate are going to put in for a transfer up to Edinburgh. And I would respectfully ask you to keep that to yourselves, sir. Chubby would go mad.'

'Would he now?' Watt said. 'That big balloon wouldn't last five minutes in Niddrie. They'd latch on to him like a leech.'

Nick looked at him. 'Then I suppose that's what it would be like for us, as constables. But it's not putting me off.' He turned right into Wauchope Place.

'Don't worry about it, son. As long as you have something upstairs, you'll be fine,' Watt said, as the car pulled into the side of the road and Nick parked behind another patrol car.

They got out into the snow which was now being driven by a strong wind that had sprung up. It was unnaturally dark, like they were heading for winter instead of spring.

There were lights on in the house. Miller thought that if this had been Edinburgh, there would have been reporters sniffing about, looking for a story. Maybe there would have been here too if it weren't for the weather. A single hack, from an obscure country paper.

He could make out a couple of uniforms in the house as they went up the path. He had to shove the gate hard to move the built-up snow.

One of the uniforms let them in. They shook their overcoats towards the open front door and stamped their feet like it was some kind of strange ritual, before being shown into the living room.

'I'm DI Miller, this is DS Watt. Are you Mrs Fitzroy's sister?'

The older woman sniffed. Nodded to the two detectives as the uniforms left the room. 'Yes. Ann Fraser. I live here too.' She shook her head. 'I can't believe she's gone. And in such a horrible way!'

One of the uniforms came in through the doorway from the kitchen with a tray filled with cups and a teapot. He put it down and started pouring.

Miller indicated for Watt to sit down. The living room was warm, the log fire sparking away behind the fireguard. The light was on in the kitchen where the uniforms were gathered.

'Mrs Fraser, I know this is a shock to you, but can you think of anybody who would want to harm your sister?'

The woman shook her head and stared into space before answering. 'No. This is hardly the drugs capital of Scotland. We don't have shootings from cars like they do in America. We don't even lock the doors on our houses, although I'm sure that will change by tonight. I can't begin to imagine why somebody would want to kill...' She broke down for a moment.

'Is there anybody special in her life? Boyfriend? Companion?' Watt asked.

Ann stopped crying and wiped her nose again. 'No. My husband died a couple of years after Ella's, so she suggested I move in here with her so we could share the bills. It worked well for us. We did everything together. We're both retired. I was a nurse, she was a teacher. We both worked in Annan but now we have...*had*...plenty of time on our hands.'

'Did either of you have any online friends? Say, on Facebook or other social media?' Miller asked.

Ann snapped her face to look at him. 'Yes! We were both on Facebook. Ella loved that. We found people we were at school with, believe it or not.'

'Can you give us the details of your pages?'

She rattled them off as Watt wrote them down.

'Did you ever see somebody get nasty on there with your sister?' Miller asked.

Ann paused for a moment. 'It's...nothing...but...' She stopped and looked at Miller.

'Go on, Mrs Fraser,' Watt said. 'It might not mean anything to you, but even a small detail can make a difference.'

Ann looked at him. 'Ella did get into a fight with a man.'

Miller sat up straight. 'On Facebook?'

'Both. You see, Ella and I are on the War Memorial Committee. So is Graham Gorman. Another man in town. He's a horrible man, always arguing about what we should do about the memorial.'

'Who's in charge of this committee?'

'He is. He thinks it's all his idea and you would think he's putting up the money out of his own pocket. Nobody likes him. But luckily we have Michael.'

'Who's Michael?'

'Michael Monro. Our new minister. Our temporary one. I wish he was staying. He's such a lovely man. He makes sure that Gorman doesn't get out of control.'

Miller could feel the warmth of the log fire grabbing hold of him. It felt comfortable and had he been here in different circumstances, he would have been happy to sit by the fire with his feet up, sipping on a whisky.

'You say Mr Gorman was arguing about the memorial, but did he make any threats to Ella?'

'Yes, sort of. Ella got the minister on her side one night when we voted about something, and he said she wouldn't get away with it.'

'How long ago was that?'

'Last week.'

'Do you know if he had any other contact with her? Like calling her?'

'He got into an argument on Facebook with her. He got nasty, using the F-word and things like that.'

'How old is he?'

'Around sixty. Something like that.'

'You said he lives in town?' Watt said.

'Yes. He also owns the bakery in the high street.'

'How many other people are on this committee?' Watt asked.

'There were six of us plus the minister. Seven in total. Gorman would always vote against Ella if we had to put something to a vote. He had a thing for her, but she didn't want to go out with him. After her husband died, she wasn't interested in other men. Gorman wouldn't take no for an answer.'

'Where can we find him?' Miller said. Watt wrote the address down.

'Do you have a phone number for the church?'

She looked it up on her phone and gave it to him.

Miller excused himself and walked through to the hall where he made a phone call before heading back into the room.

'The minister is going to meet us over at the church. He's visiting with a parishioner right now.' He looked at Ann. 'We'll go and find Mr Gorman and talk to him. I'll make sure he doesn't bother you.'

'Thank you.'

'When does the committee meet again?'

'Tomorrow night. I really want to go. Hugh Abernethy was our uncle. We never met him of course, but our mother told us the stories of how he would stay up late, writing. He was a young man but very talented. Just like Stuart, who's here for the play at the theatre.'

'We'll keep in touch, Mrs Fraser. And if there's

anything else you can think of, don't hesitate to call the station where we'll be based.'

'Thank you for coming round.'

Miller and Watt collected Nick and they left the warmth of the house to go out into what was rapidly becoming a whiteout. The snow was coming down thick and fast. They walked quickly to the Land Rover.

'To the church,' Miller said.

SEVEN

'It was simply awful,' Nancy Corbett said, putting a hand up to her brow. She turned to look at her boyfriend, actor Stuart Love. 'Hold me, Stuart. Nancy feels faint.'

Love looked at her like he was more than mildly embarrassed by her theatrical performance, but he knew if he didn't put his arms around her, then the chances of him getting any later that night were slim to none.

'There, there, my sweet.' He stepped forward and put an arm around her shoulders.

They were in the new Buccleuch Centre on Thomas Telford Road, where they would be performing at the end of the week.

'Please, sit down,' Gibb said, indicating one of the theatre's seats.

'I don't know if I can. My legs are so shaky, I might not be able to get back up again.

Gibb looked at Steffi Walker and Julie Stott; *fucking drama queen.*

'Try, Ms Corbett.'

Nancy sat down like she had piles, leaning towards Love.

'I know this is difficult, but could you please go through the events of last night,' Gibb said as he and the other two detectives sat down. He was down one row and across the aisle from them. Julie and Steffi sat in the row in front of him.

Nancy, unsurprisingly, started sobbing. Gibb could swear he saw Love's lips mouth *for fuck's sake* but he couldn't be sure in the dimmed light.

'We were here. I was rehearsing for this upcoming weekend's play,' Love said. 'We were walking back to the hotel. We walked along the riverfront and then decided to go into the playground and go on the swings. Just for a laugh. Nancy went first and then I heard her screaming. I went rushing to see what was going on, and I couldn't find Nancy. Then I saw the opening for the cemetery at the back. She was in there, standing in front of that...thing.'

'The dead woman,' Nancy said, giving her fiancé a look of distaste. 'Not a *thing*.'

'Did you hear anything in the cemetery?' Julie

asked. 'Anybody moving about?' They knew the woman had been dead for hours before she was found, but they wanted to hear the answers, to see if they would fit with what they knew.

'No. It was deadly quiet. The snow was falling. It was eerie. Places looked light when they should have been black shadows. Snow does that I suppose.'

'No sound of any engines leaving the scene?' Steffi asked.

'Nothing.'

'Did you see any cars passing by near the church?'

'Well, yes, there were a couple of cars, but they didn't stand out in any way. Like a clown car or something, would have.'

Gibb doubted there were many clown cars driving about in the town. 'Just regular traffic, in other words.'

'Exactly. If it's not a tractor, it's a Land Rover,' Nancy said, 'though Gibb knew this was an exaggeration. But the ratio of Land Rovers to head of population was probably more than Edinburgh.

'Could you see any footprints in the snow?' Steffi asked. Her face showed she was starting to tire of the dramatics.

'It was just snow,' Love said. 'If there had been footprints there, they were covered by the time we got there.'

'How long are you here for?' Gibb asked, starting to

feel the nicotine itch. He had to stop and think for a moment whether or not he had brought enough cigarettes with him. He knew if he had forgotten to bring a couple of cartons, he would end up setting fire to the curtains in his room. Anything that let off smoke. Just like a wino who would drink mouthwash.

'We have three performances this weekend; Friday, Saturday, and Sunday. Then Monday we leave. If this God-awful weather lets up, that is. The worst of it has still to come. We'll be lucky if there's more than two people at the performances, and they'll be the janitor and the cafeteria woman. I don't know why we said we'd come here.'

'It's your hometown, that's why,' Nancy said, pulling away from her fiancé. 'You said you were proud to be coming home.'

'I am, I am. But like going waterskiing naked, it sounded like a good idea at the time. But just like how I wouldn't want my baw bag slapping off a lake, I think I should have made the decision with my head, not my heart.' When Stuart Love got angry, his Scottish accent became more pronounced, something he'd spent years trying to get rid of. Like the Borders version of Sean Connery.

Nancy pulled back and slapped his arm. 'What kind of talk is this, Stuart Abernethy? Filth! You disgust me. A woman's dead and you're talking like a docker. Get out of my way. And don't bother coming to the room tonight. I don't want to see you again until rehearsal tomorrow.'

Nancy got up and ran out of the theatre.

'Trouble in paradise,' Gibb said to Julie. 'I don't think he's getting his conjugal tonight.'

'I'm sure it's a whole production when he does.'

'Nance! Don't leave!' Love got up and ran up the aisle after her.

'Piss off!' She left the theatre and stormed out, Love close on her heels.

'As interviews go, I've done better,' Gibb said.

'She looks like she needs to go over somebody's knee,' Steffi said as they left.

In the reception area, Love was standing arguing with Nancy as she put her jacket on. She stormed out into the snow.

Love turned round and looked at the detectives. 'Sorry about that. She's a bit...temperamental.'

'Mental, more like,' Steffi whispered to Julie.

'Oh yeah.'

Gibb walked over to Love. 'Your girlfriend called you *Abernethy*. I thought your name was *Love*.'

'That's my stage name. Believe it or not, there's another actor registered with the same name as me. We're not connected but I had to register another name. My mother's maiden name was Love.'

'I'm assuming you're connected to Hugh Aber-nethy in some way?'

'He was my grandfather. My father was only a baby when Hugh went missing on that plane.'

'What plane?'

'The one that went missing in Iceland during the war.'

EIGHT

Miller and Watt were waiting in the church car park with Nick behind the wheel, when the minister came speeding in, blowing snow like a plough.

'Gentlemen!' he said, grinning. 'Boy are these Landies the business, eh?' He slammed the door shut and grinned like a schoolboy. He looked to be around forty, with hair cut short and if Miller didn't know better, he would have thought the minister was a professional bodybuilder.

'Thanks for coming!' Miller shouted above the rising wind. Although only late afternoon, it looked like early evening. The street lamps had come on prematurely.

'Not at all! Let's get inside.' He walked up to the side door of the church, unlocked the door and they all stepped inside.

'Terrible business with poor Ella,' the minister said, shrugging his coat off. 'Michael Monro. Langholm's temporary minister, although by the looks of it, I don't think I'll be going anywhere any time soon. A lot of the young lads and lassies don't want to be stuck down here. They want to be up in the city.'

Miller introduced them and then he and Watt took their coats off. They followed the minister in, Nick bringing up the rear.

It was warm inside.

'Let's go through to my office where we can have a chat. I'll get the kettle on. Tea okay for everybody?'

They all agreed that tea would be just fine.

'If it's warm and doesn't taste like cat pish, it's fine,' Watt said.

'I'm sorry?' Monro said.

'I said, milk, if you have it. And some Tunnock's teacakes wouldn't go amiss.'

'Rich tea do you?'

'No thanks. If it doesn't have chocolate, I don't really participate. That's my weakness. That and lager.'

'Ah. A drinking man, Sergeant Watt.'

'I think we'll fit in just fine down here,' Miller said.

'Please, take a seat,' Monro said, moving round to the chair behind his desk after switching the kettle on.

Miller and Watt sat in other chairs, Nick remaining standing by the door.

'Can you tell me how the relationship was between Ella Fitzroy and Graham Gorman?' Miller said.

Monro shook his head and his face took on a sombre look. 'Graham is not a happy man. He's lived here all his life and doesn't take it well when somebody comes into town and gets to make decisions. Like me. Ella and I got on famously. She was a very nice woman. Mr Gorman is a cantankerous old man. Have you met him yet?'

'No, we haven't,' Watt said. 'I don't think he'll be on the welcoming committee.'

'Talking of committees,' Miller said, 'what was this war memorial one all about?'

The kettle clicked off and Monro got up and walked over to a table where the things were set up. He poured four cups of tea and dished them out. Sat back down at his desk.

'It was decided years ago that a new war memorial should be erected in the town. This was before I was sent here, of course, but money was an issue. Who was going to pay for it? So the idea went round in circles, until two months ago when the plane that Hugh Abernethy was flying in was, for all intents and purposes, spat out by a glacier.'

'I think I remember reading something about that,' Miller said.

Monro stood up. 'Come on, bring your tea with you. I'll take you through to our little meeting room.' He stood up and they followed him through to what might have been a conference room.

There were noticeboards on the walls and a table in the middle with some chairs around it. On the boards were clippings from newspapers, handwritten notes, and photos of the area.

'This is the war room, as it were,' Monro said, sipping his tea. 'It was a bit of a shambles when I got here. Nobody really knew what they were doing. I helped organise things.'

'How was it discovered?' Watt asked, looking at some of the clippings on the wall.

'Well, let me give you some background. The plane went missing in 1941. It was part of a squadron that had been transferred from France a year earlier, sent to Iceland as part of an anti-invasion force. In May 1941, Hugh Abernethy was on the plane, being flown from Melgerdi Airfield in the north, back to an airfield in Selfoss in the south. The plane never made it.

'It disappeared. Nobody knew what had happened to it. An Icelandic historian had searched for the plane many times but found nothing. His son joined him when he grew older, and when the old man died, the son would go out on his own, every so often. He hadn't been out for years and then one day he decided to look again. This time, he found the wreckage after some of the ice had melted. The plane had been missing for over seventy-five years. Nobody ever went up on that glacier, except this historian. He struck lucky one day, and then the RAF mountain rescue teams were called in. They recovered the bodies of the airmen. Hugh was eventually brought home after a ceremony in Iceland, and he's buried up in the cemetery.'

'Round the back of the church?' Watt asked.

'No, the cemetery up on the hill on the edge of town. This is an old cemetery behind here. The newer interments are all up there. In fact, when the Pan Am plane blew up, they found suitcases and clothes scattered in the cemetery up there.'

'What's all the animosity been about?'

'Ella and Ann want Hugh's name to be on its own since he's more famous.'

'And Gorman doesn't want this?' Miller said.

'Correct. He just wants Hugh's name to be the same size as everybody else's. He has an uncle who died during the war and he thinks that it's unfair. But the ladies have a famous nephew who's an actor; Stuart Love. He's the one who organised putting on his grandfather's play, to raise money for the new memorial, and the women think since their nephew is bringing in a lot of money for it, they should get their way.'

Miller drank more tea, surprised how good it was. 'Is Gorman a violent man?'

'Not since I've been here. Angry, yes, but not violent.'

Miller turned to Nick. 'You've been here longer than any of us. How well do you know Graham Gorman?'

'He's an old moan, to be honest. And he's been drunk and disorderly a few times, but when we get called out, we just take him home.'

'We're going to go and have a talk with him later. Anything we should be worried about?'

'Mr Gorman is about sixty, but don't let that fool you. He's a big man and when he's had a few, he likes to think he can take on the world.'

'Does he have access to any weapons, that you know of?' Watt said.

'Lots of farmers round here have shotguns of course, so it wouldn't surprise me if he had a shotgun. Not much call for it in his bakery, but he lives in the wilds. He prefers it that way, he says. No nosy neighbours.'

'Did you hear anything last night?' Miller said. 'After the meeting?'

'Nothing. To be honest, when the meeting was over, I went home. I'm renting a little house. When the others left, I checked the doors were locked and then left and went home.'

'Sorry to ask you this, but can anybody vouch for you?'

'Yes, Detective Miller; the big man himself.' Monro rolled his eyes heavenward.

'You've been a tremendous help, minister, and I'm sure that we'll be in touch again, for more help.'

'Call me anytime. I'm always out and about, Langholm has quite a few elderly parishioners, and it's my duty to visit them to make sure they're alright. Especially in this weather. A lot of them are elderly and don't get about so much, but I can always meet you here.'

'I understand.'

Monro walked them back to his office where they put their cups down.

Outside, more snow had landed everywhere, and Nick did his best to clear the front of their police patrol Land Rover. The minister's black one was parked right next to theirs.

'Just back to the station,' Miller said.

Nick started the big car up and drove back to the high street.

The radio crackled. Sergeant Brown letting the other members of his team know there was a bad traffic accident.

'The bridge is gone. The road leading into town from the north,' Nick said.

'What actually happened?' Miller asked.

'A petrol tanker crashed and exploded, taking the bridge down.'

NINE

London

The old man had been with the department for so long, he was known as *Skipper*. Some thought this was a term used because he had been in the navy, but they weren't sure.

Skipper sat in his office, puffing away on his pipe. Nobody ever came to his office that wasn't invited. Not anybody outside his department, anyway. Nobody complained about the smoke. Nobody would dare.

Skipper was the very embodiment of, *speak softly but carry a big stick.*

Roger Warwick was up-and-coming in the department. A young man with a fine head on his shoulders.

Skipper liked that. He trusted the young man and could see him taking the helm one day.

'There's a call waiting to be patched through from Scotland, Skipper,' Warwick said.

Skipper was looking through the window down at the Thames below. The snow was hitting the UK with a vengeance, which was going to scupper his plans for this evening with Lucy. His daughter was in the city for a visit with his grandchildren, and they had booked a table in a fine restaurant.

He turned to look at Warwick. 'Damn this weather. Bloody Russians. If they're not poisoning their agents, they're throwing their damned weather this way.' He puffed furiously for a moment. 'Who's on the phone?'

'Agent Hooper, sir.'

Skipper shook his head and groaned. 'I hope this snow isn't going to compromise the operation.'

'These are men who can be relied upon, sir.'

'I know, Roger. I hand-picked them for this job. Some of the people in this department should think themselves lucky they work for Five. They're getting too comfortable for my liking. Maybe we should get *them* out in the field. That would teach them.' He picked up the phone as Warwick retreated, closing the door behind him.

'Hooper?'

'Yes, sir. I'm calling in with a report. Is the line secure?'

'This isn't my first day on the job, Hooper. My line is secure so no matter what line you're using, it will be encrypted. Go on, I have a meeting to go to.' This meeting was with one of his cronies in one of the parliament's restaurants, but there was no need to disclose every detail.

'The bridge leading into Langholm from the north was destroyed, as planned. The weather is getting worse, but it won't stop us.'

'And bridges two and three?'

'I'd like to bring that forward. To be honest, this weather is a godsend. There isn't so much need for stealth. The traffic has been stopped further south and further north of the town. The roads are impassable.'

'How about the local force? Are they going to get in your way?'

'There's one who might be a problem, but he can be taken care of. There's also a team down from Edinburgh. There was a murder here.'

'Are *they* going to be a problem?'

Hooper laughed. 'Two old men, two young women, and a younger detective. No, sir, they will not be a problem at all.'

'Call me with regular updates. I wouldn't want the boys with the rubber soles to have to come looking for you. If they do, pray you took enough body bags for you and your team.'

'Regular as clockwork,' Hooper said, but Skipper could hear a slight change in tone. He hung up. Hooper was a good field agent, but any slight on his character, he took to heart.

The simple fact of the matter was, there was a team on stand-by, ready to pick up the pieces and clean the place up. A story was already in the pipeline to cover their own arses. The soldiers would get into the town no problem; everything was at their disposal, including skimobiles and tracked vehicles.

If Hooper and his team screwed up, the men upstairs would push the button and the black ops boys would be in. Hooper wouldn't even see it coming. Skipper knew this would not be a good thing. His team were the best fighters he knew.

He puffed on his pipe. Time for lunch. The dirty work was in good hands.

TEN

Jesse Gorman sat back in his old armchair and closed his eyes as he savoured the first whisky of the day. If his mother had still been alive, she would have been tutting at him. God bless her, he had loved her, but he would have happily killed her at times.

He rose at three forty-five every single morning except Sunday, to work in his father's bakery. He went to church on a Sunday, come rain or shine. Maybe not this Sunday coming though; rain or shine was one thing, but trudging through this fucking snow was another.

Maybe he'd stay in bed until ten. No, he couldn't. His body was conditioned for getting up early now, but it was through choice. The bakery was the best one around for miles, but only people from the town bought his stuff. Still, it made them money.

The snow was coming down like it was the end of the world. In all his life, he'd never seen anything like it. Even the snowstorm of 2010 wasn't as bad as this. Maybe the duration had been longer, but not this intensity. And God knows how long this could last. They were saying on the TV that there was no sign of it letting up. It was to get so much worse before it got better.

Normally he'd have his dinner going by now, but Pinky was coming in with the Chinese shortly. His best pal.

His father had suggested coming along to the meetings they were having about getting a war memorial put up. And he had reluctantly gone along one night, telling himself that it was on the way to the pub anyway. He had roped Pinky into it as well after the two girls started coming along.

And he had enjoyed it. Until the minister got knocked down by a car and they had to say goodbye to him. He was all for kicking it into touch after that, especially after they found the corpse of young Hugh Abernethy in Iceland.

Jesse's dad had thought it fitting that the young man's name should be included on the memorial. It hadn't been at first. Oh no, there had been talk of Abernethy being a deserter, but when they found his body in the plane wreck, that changed everything.

Including having those two old fuckers poking their noses in. They weren't interested in showing up for the meetings at first, then their uncle's body had been found and suddenly they were all over the minister like a rash.

Jesse didn't like Monro, not one little bit. He was always smiling like he was on fucking crack or something. What happened to the good old days, when the minister in the church was a hundred years old and wasn't averse to skelping some unruly child? That's how it was when he, Jesse, was a lad. By God, you spoke out of turn and the minister would take a fucking belt to your arse.

He'd been skelped on more than one occasion before the old sod had been shifted to another parish. Turns out he was dipping one of the congregation, a woman whose husband was an upstanding member of the community. The minister, who'd looked like he had been on the ark, had actually been only forty-two, but to a young boy, forty-two was a hundred and two.

You could never tell. Now this minister was the opposite. He was young and looked like he went to one of those new-fangled gyms, only they were called *health clubs* now. The only thing that got healthy from them was the owner's bank account.

Oh, I go to the health club over in Annan he heard

one of the women say to the minister, as if she was actually chatting him up. Looked like she went over to the fucking doughnut shop in Annan, more like.

But Monro was in Langholm and Jesse had taken an instant dislike to him. Like sometimes when you were introduced to the friend of a pal, and the friend looked a complete wanker. Like that. Jesse thought the minister was a complete wanker. He'd waltzed in and taken over the job of chairing the committee and everybody loved him. Jesse had offered to do it but they had all looked at him like he would dip the collection tin.

Fuck 'em all, then. Let them get on with it. Jesse would just carry on pranking the minister with the late-night phone calls. He laughed out loud at that. LOL, the youngsters called it. Fucking morons. Talking in some strange language on their phones, like they had been visited by aliens.

Jesse wasn't ancient, not by a long shot, but thirty was more mature than twelve. He wasn't averse to giving one of the little bastards a scud. Sometimes they would sit in the square over by the hospital and drink, then they would shout abuse at whoever was passing by. He'd booted one of them up the arse one day and told him to go and get his father and Jesse would boot his arse as well.

Langholm was certainly coming into the 21st

century. Hooligans – kids telling you to fuck off with the same nonchalance as saying *good morning*.

Thank God he had Pinky in his life. Who should be here any minute now.

'Starting without me?' George *Pinky* Malone said, coming into the house, as if on cue.

'Grab yourself a glass. How's the roads?'

'Shite. I thought I was going to go over the Telford bridge and I don't mean across it.'

'We'll have to toss a coin to see who goes for the Chinese.'

'Are ye blind, ye daft bastard? What have I got in my hand?'

'Usually your willy, but on this occasion, I'll guess it's something to eat or drink.'

'Correct and correct. Chinese in the carrier bag, whisky and cans of lager in the car. I think we might have to hunker down.'

'Aye, it's a bastard right enough.'

'I'll bet everybody is having to stay with somebody. Those daft enough to go out on the pish are going to find themselves stranded.'

'I'm certainly not going out to the boozer in this. I'd probably fall off the footbridge, knowing me.'

'Aye, you're a clumsy wank-muffin at the best of times.'

'Cheeky fucker. Get your coat off, you're dripping all over my best shag.'

'It could do with a spot of water on it. Just add some shampoo and you'll see the pattern again.' Pinky put the food on the table in the living room and took his jacket off, hanging it on a hook on the back of the door.

Jesse chugged his own whisky back and got up to pour himself another and Pinky his first. 'What's with that daft boot getting herself murdered?'

'I don't think she had a hand in it.'

'I'm not saying that, but if some bastard came at me in the cemetery, I'd boot his clacker bag across his forehead.'

'Aye, well, I don't think Ella was in any position to fight off who was attacking her. Anyway, I thought you liked her?'

'Not in that way. She was an old moan.'

'Respect for the dead, and all that.' Pinky accepted the glass of whisky.

'I tell you what, I bet those two lassies are shiting themselves.'

'And that's why we have to strike while the iron's hot. Move in there.'

'What do you mean?'

Pinky rolled his eyes. 'Listen to him. Acting all innocent, as if he hasn't had the same thoughts as me.'

Jesse stared at his friend. 'Are you on drugs?'

Pinky laughed. 'No, but what we're after is better than drugs. Let's get the scran going and I'll tell you. Go and get the beer from the car.'

They dished out the food and sat at the old table after Jesse had been out to the car.

'Last night, a woman was murdered, which has put everybody on edge. Including the two lassies from the committee.'

Jesse put food into his mouth and nodded as if he understood. Then he belched loudly.

'Fuck's sake, that's not going to make Mary want to come back to your place.'

'It's this cheap fucking lager.'

'Nothing cheap about it, the price that old fanny in the store charges. Anyway; that old boot is murdered and now the women in the town are looking over their shoulders. There's a nutter here and nobody knows who he is.'

'It could be you, for all I know,' Jesse said.

'And I'm staying here tonight. You might wake up with your nob in your mouth.'

'As I long as I don't wake up with *your* nob in my mouth.'

'Try and stay on track here, Gormy. Mary and Isabel are good fun, right? Like to party and get pished. But right now, they need protection. That's where we step in.'

Jesse still looked blank.

'Look, what if we called them, from another phone of course, or one of those throwaway jobbies?'

'A throwaway jobby? What the fuck is that?'

'Were you dropped on your heid when you were a bairn?'

'Probably.'

'We call them. They start to think they're being targeted. Suddenly, they want us to take them everywhere. Including back here to your place.'

'They think we're like bodyguards or something?' said Jesse.

'Now you're getting it.'

'You hope to get into Isabel's good books by scaring the fuck out of her. I don't want to sound like a killjoy, but that plan has flaws.'

'No it doesn't. See, what we have to do, is walk them home from the meeting tomorrow night, but before that, we can call them up and tell them they're being watched. A bit of heavy breathing.'

Jesse shook his head. 'The best we can hope for is to share a prison cell, so we don't have to get married to a stranger.'

'Oh don't talk pish. All we're going to do is put the wind up them. They already said they would go to see the play with us on Friday. This way, they'll be only too glad to hang on to our arms. And other things once we get them back here.'

'Or your place.'

'My mother never leaves the house,' Pinky said.

'Christ, we're not doing any harm. Just making sure the women appreciate us.'

'I don't know. As plans go, it's not waterproof.'

'How so?'

'If they find out, the last thing we'll be getting is our rock 'n' roll. We'll be getting ten years.'

Pinky laughed. 'You worry too much, Gormy.'

'Like the bank job?'

'Hey, hey, we'll have none of that talk. I'm a reformed man. I don't plan things like that anymore. Besides, I wasn't really trying to rob the place. I was just trying to make a point that they're all greedy bastards.'

Now it was Jesse's turn to laugh. 'The note was a joke as well, was it? *Give me your cash?* You didn't count on it being that teller's time of the month. What did she say to you again?'

'Never mind.'

Jesse laughed more. 'Come on, tell me.'

'*Fuck off you little twat or I'll snap you in two.*'

Jesse sprayed beer all over the table and then laughed hysterically. 'Just as well you didn't get caught or you not only would have got away empty-handed, but more than likely got a belting off a lassie into the bargain.'

Pinky sat back, shook his head, and took a swig from the can, waiting for his friend to calm down. 'This is different. Just a wee phone call. It's nothing worse than you calling the minister.'

'Okay then. I'm on board, but where are we going to get a throwaway phone in Langholm?'

Pinky put his bottle on the table and went over to where his overcoat was hanging. He reached into a pocket and brought out a phone. 'I was in Carlisle today. Almost got fucking stranded, too. Daft bastard driver said he might not be able to go north because of the snow. A few threats and he was on the road.'

'Did you buy it off him or something?'

'Fuck sake, Gormy. Get a grip of yourself. I went into one of those fucking rip-off merchants who try and sell you a fancy phone. I told the boy to bog off and just give me a throwaway phone as I'd lost my other one.'

'And he gave you it, just like that?'

'I had to buy it, dafty. It wasn't like he was handing them out.'

'You sure it's legit?' Jesse played with the phone as if it would explode any second.

'Of course. The preferred phones of bank robbers everywhere.'

Jesse laughed. 'You should have kept your other one, from when you went into the bank.'

'Oh fuck off, Gormy.'

'Alright, I'm kidding.'

'So we just make a call, saying nothing at first.'

'You do it. Then I want to call the minister.'

ELEVEN

'You should try this shepherd's pie,' Paddy Gibb said, tucking into his dinner. 'Oh, I forgot; you can't 'cause you're not staying here. What did you boys have for dinner?'

'That's abuse of power, just so you know,' Andy Watt said. 'But do you know how they make shepherd's pie? They scrape all the bits off the butcher's floor and cover it in potatoes. Like innards and eyeballs.'

Gibb shrugged. 'Stop talking pish and get me another beer.'

'You know, any other human being would have thrown his ring at that piece of imparted wisdom. You're just an animal.'

The five of them were sitting round one of the

tables in the Eskdale dining room, away from other patrons.

'Here you are, gentlemen,' a young waitress said, bringing three more shepherd's pies for Miller, Watt and Steffi.

'Thank you,' Miller said, looking at his food, his imagination running wild as to what the contents were. He looked at Watt. 'And before you say something else, if I bring this dinner back up later, it will be in your room.'

'Really?' Steffi said. 'You two plan on spending time with each other after hours?' She grinned at them.

'Oh, you're such a comedian, Sergeant Walker. But remember that reports will be written up in Edinburgh, and I will be sure to spell your name correctly,' said Miller.

'Aw, sir, I was only joking.'

'No you weren't.'

'You're right, I wasn't.'

'Make sure you pay that lassie for the meals. Julie and I get ours included, but you three have to pay.' Gibb forked more food into his mouth. 'What's wrong with the food in the boarding house?'

'Have you been in there? The wallpaper looks more appetising than her menu. There's two dishes to choose from; stew or vegetarian stew, which is stew without the beef in it.'

'I'm sure it's good healthy food.'

'I'll put your name down for breakfast then, will I?'

'There's no need to be insubordinate, Sergeant Watt. There are children in Africa who would enjoy such a meal.'

'I thought you were both going to use the Chinese?' Julie Stott said.

'The old closet said we couldn't bring it back to her place. I suppose the thought of real food being in her dining room would cause a riot. Those poor sods who live there for weeks at a time must think it's just one step up from prison. In fact, they probably get better scran in Saughton.'

A man came across with a tray; three pints of lager and two soft drinks. Gibb indicated that it should be put on his tab.

'Wow, you actually have a tab going?' Watt said.

'Police Scotland are picking up that one too. It will be put under *sundries* the owner told me,' Gibb said.

'Good job.'

'Only soft drinks, ladies?' Miller said.

'We might have to drive.'

'Good call.' He raised his glass and for a split second, felt guilty that he was miles from home, enjoying a beer with his colleagues instead of being at home, helping to look after his new baby daughter.

'How did the questioning go with Stuart Love?' he asked Gibb.

Gibb swallowed his food. 'God, that lassie he's got himself hooked up with must be an aspiring actress, let me tell you. Bloody drama queen. I don't know what he sees in her.'

'She looks different in real life than from the photos in the papers.'

'I know Love was in that stupid soap on TV, but he's not really a big name. Is he?' Watt said.

'If you switched channels more often, you'd see him on more things,' Gibb said. 'Even I know who he is. He was on *Celebrity Big Brother*.'

'I don't watch that.'

'Have you seen that show, Miller?' Gibb said, putting his knife and fork down on the empty plate and pushing it away.

'I have.'

'See, Andy? Even Frank has a bit of culture about him.'

'I prefer to watch sport.'

'Drinking's not a sport.' Gibb drank some of his lager. 'So what we have so far is, Love and his new flame were at the theatre, which has been confirmed, and they walked along to the playground. Then the girlfriend saw the corpse nailed to the tree.'

'Ella's sister said she got into a spat with another committee member,' Miller said. 'A man called Graham Gorman.'

'We have an address for him, I assume?'

'He lives up the road from the church. Nick Jones gave me directions.'

'And he was slagging her off on Facebook, too,' Watt said, chugging down some lager.

'Plenty of those trolls slag people off when they're hiding behind a keyboard,' Steffi said.

'That's how you met your boyfriend, isn't it, Steffi?' Watt said. 'Stalking him on Facebook?'

'Sod off.'

'Basically, all we have is an angry committee member. I think we'll go and pay him a visit. Andy, why don't you and I go through some paperwork with Julie, while Frank and Steffi go talk to this guy?'

'Fine by me. I don't like driving in this anyway.'

'You can drive,' Gibb said to Steffi. 'Miller will have you through somebody's living room if he drives.'

'I used to be world rally champion on the Nintendo,' Miller retorted.

Gibb drank some more lager and shook his head. 'He doesn't even go red when he lies. Just try and come back in one piece. If you need us, give us a bell here at the hotel and I'll have that big shagger drive us over.'

'Will do.'

'See? Aren't you glad she's only having a Coke?'

'I looked into my crystal ball,' Steffi said.

'I'm glad you're into witchcraft. That's how Miller drives; using black magic.'

TWELVE

The B709 was a narrow, two-lane country road that went from Langholm to Lockerbie, Eskdalemuir, and the Tibetan Centre.

A mile out of town was a layby on the left, opposite a guardrail that bordered an embankment on the edge of the River Esk. Telephone poles carried wires into the town from the west.

A JCB with council markings on it had been sitting in the layby with a pile of gravel in front of it and three huge boulders, as if it was waiting to do some job. There were traffic cones and some metal signs sitting nearby, now all covered in snow.

Nobody looked at it twice, nobody questioned it. Even as the snow fell harder and started to cover the big, yellow machine, nobody even gave it a second glance.

Now there was no traffic travelling up or down the road because of the weather. Except for the black Land Rover Defender, short wheelbase.

Probably nobody would have questioned them either unless they were questioning their sanity for being out in this. But the two men in the vehicle were confident nobody would come along.

Considering they had both been Royal Marines Commandos before joining Five, it wouldn't be a problem. 'You got the keys for that thing?'

'You asked me that before we left the house. Just like my ex-wife used to ask me if I'd remembered to put the fucking cooker off when we were on a night out.' He rifled about in his pockets for the keys and brought them out.

'This was a bit of luck, this weather.'

'We couldn't have asked for better cover. We would have still got the job done, but this helps us so we don't have to be so stealthy.'

'Money for old rope. Remember the days in the SBS? Man, I miss that so much.'

'How could I forget? Best days of our lives, mate.' Hooper sat and looked out of the windscreen at the heavy snow that was coming down in front of them, dancing through the headlight beams. 'This is what makes it all worthwhile. Doing stuff like this.'

'*Field Operations Managers*. That's what we're called. As long as they wrap it up the way they want it, they can sleep at night.'

'Best of both worlds though; they get the job done, and we get to carry on as if we were still in the service.'

'And we get better paid for it,' Smart said, laughing.

Hooper stared out of the window again for a moment, then he nudged his friend on the arm. 'Let's do it.'

Hooper got out of the warmth of the car and took a broom out of the back before walking over to the big JCB wheel loader. It was a large machine with a huge bucket on the front. He swept as much of the snow as he could off the cab before tossing the broom aside and climbing up into the cab. The machine started first time with a roar. He switched the lights on and those beams too bounced off the falling snow.

Hooper lifted the big bucket on the front and then turned the machine a bit, lowering the bucket and using it to lift snow out of the way, essentially digging himself out. He drove the machine across the road, the huge tyres digging into the snow like it wasn't even there.

The engine roared as Hooper lifted the bucket until he was next to a telephone pole. Then he put the bucket against the side of the pole and pushed.

The pole came crashing down, bringing the wires with it. It fell down the embankment into the river below. Then Hooper brought the machine back and pushed against the guardrail, which succumbed to the pressure from the big machine. The metal supports were ripped from the ground as the guardrail went the same way as the pole. Hooper was backing up to move down to get at more rail when he stopped.

Smart saw the lights from the car at the same time.

The road was twisty and had it been a dry, summer's day, the car would have been on them before they knew it, but as it was, the road was covered in snow and the other Land Rover was making slow progress, but progress nonetheless, its headlight beams cutting a swathe through the snow.

Hooper stopped the JCB in the middle of the road and sat waiting for the car to approach.

The driver pulled up close to the machine. Hooper looked over to their own Land Rover, and although he couldn't see his friend, he knew he would be on full alert.

The driver got out of the other vehicle and walked slowly up to the JCB. He was shouting something to Hooper, but Hooper just sat and stared at him.

The wheel loader was a huge machine and dwarfed the man. He seemed to ignore the Land Rover sitting by the pile of gravel as if he didn't see Smart inside it.

Smart watched the man shouting and waving his arms about. Then he climbed on the steps that led up to the cab, and Smart thought it was time to intervene. He stepped out of his vehicle and walked across to the JCB. The man had stepped back down when he saw the driver wasn't getting out.

The wind fought the noise of the diesel engine, so Smart had to shout.

'What's up?'

The man turned round. 'What the hell is going on?'

'The road's blocked.'

'I can bloody well see that! That idiot in there is blocking it! What the hell is he doing?'

'He's new. He'll get the hang of it.'

The man looked incredulous. 'New? He's a fucking idiot. Get him out of there. Are you his boss?'

'Yes.' Smart waved up to Hooper. The big engine went quiet, leaving only the wind to make a noise as it drove the snow.

The man turned round as Hooper opened the cab door. 'What the bloody hell do you think you're doing?'

Smart stepped forward and took the cosh out of his pocket and smacked the man hard on the temple. The man crumpled to the ground.

'Help me get him into the back of our car.' Hooper grabbed the man's legs as Smart grabbed him under the armpits and they moved him into their Land Rover. 'We'll put him with the other one.'

They carried him to their Land Rover and took a petrol can and rag out of the back. Opened the other man's bonnet and splashed some petrol on the engine, jammed the rag into a crevice, poured some petrol on it and then lit it before jumping back.

'Right my friend, do your stuff.'

Hooper went back to the huge machine, turned the engine back on and positioned it at the side of the Land Rover and rammed it as the flames were licking out from under the bonnet. The big car went over the embankment sideways, before stopping against a tree.

The fire increased in intensity before the car exploded in a fireball.

Smart looked at his friend sitting in the cab and waved him forward. He put the petrol can off to one side. Even when they found the wreck, they wouldn't know if anybody was still inside or not. And when they found it empty, they would search for him, assuming he had got out and maybe dropped down in the snow. Either way, they wouldn't find him. Not yet.

The loader picked up the first boulder and laid it across the road. It was four-foot-high and weighed a tonne. The other two were similar in size, and the three of them sitting next to each other on the road was enough to block any traffic that should come down.

When Hooper was finished, he stopped the machine, keeping it pointing towards the embankment. Smart came over with the can and they opened the engine cover, splashing the remaining petrol on the engine.

The flames from the burning Land Rover lit up the area down by the river. As Smart finished pouring petrol over the engine, Hooper started the machine up again, put it into gear and jumped out, landing in the soft snow.

They watched as the flames licked out from under the engine cover, and it made a loud boom as it toppled over the edge of the embankment and crashed through the trees, going towards the river. Then it exploded, lighting up the night sky.

'Come on, let's go.'

They got into the Land Rover. Nobody gave it a second glance. Even if some over-zealous copper called it in, it would show it belonged to the highway department. Five had added the vehicle to the list of vehicles that were registered to the highway department.

'It feels good to be out in the field, doesn't it?' Hooper said.

'I don't know what I would do with my life if I wasn't causing mayhem.'

He laughed as he drove back into town.

'It's not quite holding a sniper rifle, but it's a close second.' He looked round to check the other man was still unconscious.

Hooper smiled in the darkness as they drove through the relentless snow.

THIRTEEN

Miller and Steffi walked across to the Land Rover parked in front of the town hall, Steffi putting her arm through his. 'If I'm going down, I want a soft landing,' she said to him as he smiled.

'With all this country cooking, I'm sure I'll have put on a few pounds by the time I go home.'

'You must work out though, DI Miller?'

'Call me Frank when we're not doing business. God knows, everybody else does. And when do I get time to work out?'

The snow was still falling. The plough hadn't been back along the road but there were some tyre tracks in the middle of the road, some valiant driver trying to make it to somewhere.

Steffi backed the car out of the space, the tyres cutting easily through the snow.

'Can I ask you something, Steffi?'

She looked at him in the darkness of the car. 'Sure. Ask me anything.'

She turned the car and drove along the high street. It was devoid of any traffic as the headlight beams cut through the darkness, although they could easily see after the snow had filled in the blanks.

'After Mr Blue took you that time, does it have any effect on you? I mean, do you get nightmares or anything?'

She thought about it for a moment. 'Sometimes. I deal with it though.' She said the last part as if she had realised that she had said something out of turn and it was going to come back and bite her.

'I believe you.'

'Why do you ask? Is it something I've done?'

'Oh God, no.' He stared out of the windscreen as the snowflakes came down hard and fast at them. Little pieces of frozen water that would hit them and conspire to cause mayhem before eventually dying. Like some people Miller had had the misfortune to come across in his career.

He looked at her again. 'I just wondered if I was the only one.'

'What do you mean, sir? Frank.'

'I died in the underground garage. The paramedics brought me back. I didn't know it then of course. I was well out of it. But when I lie awake at night and think of what might have happened, I start to shake.'

'Have you spoken to the force psychologist about this? Harvey Levitt is a remarkable man.'

He looked out the front of the car again as Steffi navigated it over the Thomas Telford bridge, the river roaring below in the darkness. The wipers battled against the storm. Miller thought the snow coming at them was like Captain Kirk standing on the bridge of the Enterprise and watching the stars coming at him through the windows. Never-ending. Relentless.

'Harvey is a good man. He helped me deal with Carol's death. But I don't want to bother him with this. He's a busy man and this is trivial.'

'You wake up sweating, thinking about what might have happened if something different had happened, or if somebody hadn't got there in time?'

His nod was barely perceptible. 'Yes. I hate to admit it. I'm supposed to be a man, and men are macho. We can deal with anything, especially more than a woman can.' He looked at her. 'And if you believe that pish, you'll believe anything. Women are so much smarter and better at dealing with things than men ever will be. I'm the first to admit that. I wish I had your strength. The truth is, I don't. This so-called macho man is a shaking wreck at times.'

'Have you told Kim about this?'

'No. She's a lot tougher than I am, and I think it's just male pride that's stopping me.' He smiled at her, a smile that could have been described as a grimace in other circumstances. 'Let's keep this conversation between ourselves, okay?'

'You got it, boss. I am in no hurry to admit that I cry sometimes. I want my career to go a lot further, and I don't want to be held back by some cretin who thinks that women shouldn't be in a man's position.'

'I think most of those dinosaurs are gone now. And I don't doubt for one minute that you'll be as high as Jeni Bridge one day, if not higher.'

'Andy Watt's still around.' She turned left into Henry Street, past the old police station, which was being refurbished. A lone light was shining upstairs.

'Let me tell you something about Andy Watt; he's a pain in the arse. He will talk disrespectfully to Paddy Gibb, and me of course, and he'll run away at the mouth. But he will never, and I stress this, never mean anything by it. He'll say things to people who don't know him that might sound offensive, but he will always have your back. If you got into a fight, he would be the first one there, and his attitude is, if he gets a kicking, somebody else is at least going home with a sore face.

'I would trust that man with my life. He will be your best friend. He would never drop you in it to advance himself. He's a hundred per cent reliable and he will always be by your side. Don't let the wisecracks fool you. He'll only slag you off if he likes you.'

They headed along the quiet street of terraced houses. Past a little grocer's shop on a corner. At the end, they could hardly make out the houses facing them as the road turned round to the right. Even though the Defender was a big car, it still managed to go sideways as Steffi took the turn, before she expertly corrected it.

'Wait 'til I tell Gibb you nearly had us through somebody's living room.'

'Ha. You wish.'

'We go up here and it's a house set back from the main road, as it goes round to the left, according to PC Jones,' Miller said.

It took five minutes to get there. The house was set back from the road a bit. They drove into the driveway, up the incline and round to the left. The road was more of a track than anything else. Steffi parked next to a smaller Land Rover Defender.

'This place is too isolated for me,' she said, beginning to sweat. 'I wouldn't like to live outside of town.'

'Me neither.' Miller looked out past the swiping wiper blades and didn't see any sign of life. The house was in darkness. 'I hope he's home.'

'There were no tyre tracks coming down here, but

it's coming down so fast, it probably would have covered anything.'

'I wonder why they all drive dark ones, instead of bright red?'

'If it's for a farm, I doubt they sell many in red.'

They got out.

'Let's see if he's in or if we had a wasted trip.'

Nick Jones was putting his leather jacket on in the changing room when Brown came in.

'Where are you off to?' Brown asked.

'Off home. It's been a long day.'

'Indeed you are not.'

Nick made a face. 'What?'

'I need you to do a job for me.'

'And what would that be? Feed your pet hedgehog?'

'Don't get lippy with me.'

Nick held his tongue in place. If he'd had any reservations about applying for Edinburgh, then they dissipated in a heartbeat.

'I'm off the clock.'

'Just remember, sonny, you'll need a reference for Edinburgh.'

'How did you...?'

'I know everything.'

'What is it you want?'

Brown smiled. 'That's better. You drive one of those Japanese rice-cooking things, don't you? With the four-wheel drive.'

For fuck's sake. 'Yes, the Japanese version of the British cars, except they don't break down. Maybe if the workers actually spent quality time building them instead of arsing around, we'd have better cars. My father told me all about British Leyland.'

'Alright, son, I wasn't mentioning that to get you wound up. I just want to know you'll be okay to do a bit of driving in it.'

'It gets me where I want to go. Even in this weather.'

'Good to know. I need you to follow those reprobates from Edinburgh. See where they're going.'

'Haven't they told you?'

'They're keeping their cards close to their chest. I don't like that. Not in my town.'

Fucking old sweetie wife. 'Okay.'

'Get a move on then. They've just left in one of the Landies. With that lassie driving it. I hope they don't fuck it up.'

Nick was imagining sending his transfer request the following day as he left the station and got into his car at the back of the station. He watched as the Land

Rover turned onto the bridge further along the road. His four-wheel drive made mincemeat of the snow.

He had to admit he was curious as to where they were going.

Miller and Steffi took out a flashlight each and shone it around the front of the property. Nothing seemed out of place. They walked over to the front door and knocked, but there was no response after a few minutes.

'Keep your eyes open, Steffi. If this our guy, he's strong, strong enough to hold up a woman and hammer nails into her hands.'

'You don't think he acted alone, do you?'

'What makes you say that?'

'Because I think the same thing. One or more had to be holding her while the other hammered the nail. And I'm sure she was screaming, but nobody on Caroline Street heard anything? The houses are just across from the graveyard.'

'You're right. I was starting to think that somebody held and gagged her while somebody else hammered the nails.'

'If there *is* more than one person doing this, why?'

'It's a lot more than just an argument over a war

memorial,' Miller said. 'Come on, let's see what's going on round the back.'

They trudged round, their boots sinking into the snow. Nothing had been shovelled or disturbed. They turned round the corner and walked up to the back door. Knocked again. Steffi looked in through the kitchen window and shone her flashlight in, putting a hand up to the glass so she could see inside.

Miller tried the door handle. The door opened. Nobody in Langholm locked their door, Ann Fraser had told him.

'Call Gibb. Let him know what we're doing.'

'Yes, sir.' She took her phone out and dialled Gibb's number while Miller opened the door wider.

Steffi ended the call and they took their batons out.

'If I don't call back in five minutes, he'll get Brown and the uniforms over here.'

Miller nodded and they stepped inside. He fumbled for a light switch, and to his surprise, the kitchen light came on.

Nothing looked out of place. They were about to go upstairs when Miller noticed something.

Miller switched his flashlight off.

'Steffi, go and put the kitchen light off, quick!' Miller said, reaching for the living room switch. Steffi ran back and slapped the light switch and put off her own flashlight, throwing the house back into darkness.

'What is it, sir?'

'Somebody's creeping about outside. I think he's coming round the back.' He indicated for her to stand on one side of the doorway, while he stood on the other. A few seconds later, they both heard the footsteps crunching through the snow. He didn't know if it was old man Gorman coming back or not.

A flashlight shone in through the kitchen doorway, the beam slicing through to the living room. They heard boots on the tile floor, the light getting closer.

'Let me see your fucking hands!' Miller shouted, switching his flashlight on and raising his baton, just as Steffi raised hers.

'Fuck me!' Nick Jones said, lifting his own baton.

'Jesus, Jones, what the fuck are you doing here?' Steffi said, recognising the man.

Miller put the light back on. 'Christ, I nearly gave you a belting there,' Miller said. 'What the hell are you doing here?'

Nick looked uncertain for a second. 'Look, I don't want to be here. I was about to go home when Brown said I had to follow you guys. And you might as well hear it from me, but I am about to put in a transfer up to Edinburgh, me and my pal, and Brown found out about it, so he's basically blackmailing me. But I saw the lights come on, so I thought you wouldn't be able to see out the windows, and I thought I'd come and see what was going on. Look, sir, I know it's wrong, but I don't want to be stuck down here with Brown...'

Miller held up a hand. 'Never mind, Brown. He's obviously a halfwit who will be getting his proverbial nuts kicked in the morning.'

'Sir, look, please, I don't want to cause trouble. My career will be down the toilet if I do that.'

Miller looked at the man and he remembered how it was when he himself had started out. 'Okay, but I don't like being spied on. We'll sort something out. Help us search the rest of the house. Let's see if he's upstairs.'

They went up and searched the bedrooms, but the house was empty.

There was no sign of the old man.

'Do you know Gorman at all?' Steffi asked.

'Everybody knows everybody in this town. In the few months I've been here, I know everybody by name now.'

'Does he have any family?'

'His wife is dead, but his son has a little house a few streets over.'

'You know the address?' Miller said.

'Yes.'

'There's nothing else we can do here. I'll give Brown a call. And don't worry, he won't be giving you any grief.'

Miller took out his phone and called the station. Brown answered it.

'This is DI Miller. I'm here with Constable Jones. I'm seconding officer Jones to my team. He'll be working for me, not you. Is that clear?'

'Yes.' Brown hung up.

'That man has a bad attitude, let me tell you. But you're working with me for the duration of this investigation. Wear civvies like us. If Brown doesn't like it he can deal with it. And for God's sake, don't go creeping up on us like that again.'

FOURTEEN

Paddy Gibb pulled up the collar of his overcoat as he and Andy Watt stepped out from the hotel round to the Thomas Hope Hospital, just round the corner. 'Just be on your best behaviour.'

'I resent that. I'm always the consummate professional.'

'Don't use words you can't spell, son. And not too fast or else I'll bring that fucking pie back up. That wouldn't look too good in front of this doctor, blowing my dinner all over her shoes.'

'Jesus, you're giving me the fucking boak just picturing that, Paddy. That would be a laugh though, seeing you on your hands and knees blowing chunks about the floor. That one would be up on Facebook in a minute.'

'You better not be putting stuff on there. This is business we're here on.'

'Pish. Even coppers have to get some downtime.'

'Just don't make it look like we're having a good time, for God's sake. Jeni Bridge will be scouring your page for any sign of hilarity.' They entered through the gates onto the hospital ground.

'This is your idea of hilarity? Walking about in a bloody snowstorm, still working when we should be sitting in front of that fire in your hotel, savouring the best of what Scotland has to offer? Your idea of partying is a wee bit different from mine.'

'I have to admit, I'd rather be sitting in the snug of *The Gravediggers* with Maggie than be down here.'

'See? Old dog!'

'Between you and me, I enjoy her company. She's a good laugh.'

'I knew it! Mind, she's not my cup of tea, but I bet she gives a good—'

'Hey, we're companions, for God's sake,' Gibb interrupted. 'It's not like that.'

'I was going to say *back rub*, if you could keep your mind out of the gutter for a minute, Paddy.'

'I'm too long in the tooth for this. I should be paid danger money, working with you.'

They went inside, into the warmth, brushing snow off their heads. 'Listen, if Maggie Parks puts your car in gear, then so be it. There's nothing wrong with her. Just because I wouldn't, you know, take her dancing or something, that doesn't mean to say you can't step out for the odd waltz with her.'

'Christ, I can't get my head round whether you're actually talking about dancing or shagging here.'

'As long as you know the difference when the time comes, you'll be laughing.'

They made their way down to Dr Eve Ross's office. She wasn't in there but in the mortuary.

Gibb stood at the door of the refrigeration room and knocked. 'DCI Gibb with the photos you requested,' he said.

'In case she mixes you up with the toy boy she's expecting,' Watt said in a low voice.

'Shut up, for God's sake,' Gibb said in an even lower voice.

Eve stood in the refrigeration room, looking down at Ella Fitzroy's unseeing eyes.

'I'm sorry to drag you in here on your evening off, Chief Inspector,' Eve said.

'We're on call twenty-four hours when we're down here. It's not as if we're on holiday. And call me Paddy.' He'd already made up his mind that he was going to call her Eve, no doubt fuelled by the couple of pints he'd had with dinner.

The doctor smiled at him. 'Okay, Paddy.' Eve was

wearing black jeans and a sweatshirt, with a lined hoody. 'And your friend DS Watt is with you.' She smiled a warm smile at Watt.

'Good to see you again, doctor.'

'Likewise, Andy.'

'What made you come in here tonight and look at the victim again?' Gibb asked, as he and Watt took their coats off and hung them on a coat rack.

'This damn weather. Our victim should have been down in Dumfries by now, at their new Royal Infirmary. Instead, she's stuck here, so I've arranged to talk to the head pathologist online.' She smiled at him. 'Thank you for bringing the crime scene photos in.'

'That's what we're here for, Eve.' He glanced at her, pleased that she didn't object to him using her name.

Eve's iPad made a sound, indicating a caller wanted to Facetime with her. She answered it and smiled at the man on the other end.

'Thank you for getting back to me, Simon. I have DCI Paddy Gibb here with me, and DS Andy Watt.' Again, she smiled at Watt. 'Paddy, Andy, this is head pathologist, Professor Simon Larking, Dumfries Royal Infirmary.' She turned the tablet to face the two men, and they saw a man of indeterminate age standing looking at him in a well-lit mortuary.

'Hello, detectives. I hope you're enjoying Langholm.'

'We have beer and whisky here, so it's not all bad,' said Watt, grinning.

'We're hoping to catch a show at the end of the week,' Gibb said.

'*He* is. I'll be propping up the bar.'

Gibb nudged him and Eve laughed and turned the tablet away. 'Paddy brought photos. I also have the victim out for viewing. I appreciate you going over this with me, Simon.'

'No problem. Show me the victim first, then I'd like to see the photos of when she was found.'

Their own room was well lit, and Eve held the iPad up, camera facing the opposite way so Simon could see Ella's corpse.

'Just a bit closer to her throat,' Simon said, while Gibb looked on. 'That's it. Hold it there for me, Eve.'

Gibb stood in silence. This place was like any other hospital he'd ever been in; the smell was universal. He wondered how people who worked in hospitals coped with the smell. It wasn't sitting well with his shepherd's pie.

'Now, move the camera down to each hand. Let me see each palm. You said the nails went right through, but I want to see each entry wound.'

Eve looked at Gibb. 'Could you put gloves on and turn her hands over for me, please, Paddy?'

Gibb was well practised in the art of snapping latex gloves on. A second later, he was turning Ella's left hand over. Eve moved the camera in.

'Next hand, Eve,' Simon said.

They both moved round to the other side of the table where Gibb turned the right hand over.

'Okay, Eve, I want you to show me each of the photos in turn.'

'Okay, I'm taking you over to the table.'

Eve walked over to a work table, Gibb following like a little puppy dog. Watt stood behind them. The photos had been spread out in the order they had been taken.

The snow, the graveyard. The corpse. Eve walked up to the first photo of Ella's body as it had been hanging by her hands.

Simon was looking at them and told Eve when to move on to the next one.

When they came to the last one, Eve stood up straight, stretching her back and responding to Gibb's unspoken enquiry. 'An old injury,' she said. 'I used to do wrestling in college and it went bad one training day.'

'Really?' Gibb said, not sure what to follow that up with, so he didn't bother.

Eve laughed. 'I slipped down some icy steps. Wrestler indeed. Do I look like a bloody wrestler?'

Gibb could hear Simon laughing. 'I dunno, Eve, I heard you were a pretty good wrestler in college. Well, it's a sort of wrestling, isn't it?' More laughter.

'Cheeky bugger. What do you think of this, Paddy?'

'I'm saying nothing.'

Eve laughed again and handed him her iPad. 'Would you mind doing the honours?'

'Of course not.' He took the tablet from her and showed the photos to Simon.

After they were done, Gibb put the tablet on the table and the three of them pulled up a rolling stool and sat down in front of the camera.

Simon was looking at them. 'From what I've seen, and bearing in mind I'm not actually there, I'm thinking that Ella Fitzroy was crucified post-mortem.'

'I was thinking that myself, but I wanted to see the crime scene photos again,' Eve said.

'There was no blood on her hands from the nails being hammered through,' Gibb said. 'Right?'

'Correct, Paddy,' Simon said.

'If that's the case,' Watt said,' then it's a good bet there was more than one of them. One to hold her corpse up and one to bang the nails in.'

Eve turned to look at him. 'Christ, I was just

thinking about her from a medical point of view, but if that is the case, then that's even scarier than I thought.'

'What's even scarier is, they're still on the loose,' Simon said.

'Thanks for your help, Simon. I really appreciate it,' Eve said. They disconnected and Eve put her iPad away.

'You boys going back to the hotel?'

'To the bar, yes. Some of my other officers are out but we'll head back.' He scooped up the photos and put them back in the envelope.

'You don't mind if I join you?' Eve said.

'First one's on Andy,' Gibb replied.

FIFTEEN

'I think I'm going to have a hot shower then get into my PJs,' Hooper said. 'I need to unwind.'

''PJs? What, you turn into a woman?'

'Shut up. I feel knackered. We've had a busy day. Blowing up a tanker, destroying a road. *And* I'm going to have a lie-in tomorrow.'

'We'll see about that, my old son. Team meeting tomorrow morning.'

'Not at the crack of dawn.'

'We're still going to have to go searching, remember?'

'I'm sure the old fella will have thought about things overnight, and by breakfast tomorrow, he'll be wanting to sing.'

They took their work gear off and walked through to the back of the house. 'Get the kettle on, cock.'

'Remember the days when we would slip out of a boat and go underwater and then pop up silently and blow some fucker away?'

'Yeah, them was the good old days.'

Their phone rang. The satellite one. It was Skipper, from London.

'Good evening, sir,' Hooper said.

'I'm off to my club in a minute, but I'm calling to see how things are going there. The head of our department is breathing down my neck, hence I'm now breathing down yours.'

'Sir, the bridge on the north end of town is gone, after the petrol tanker explosion. We've just blocked the main road in from the west. Tomorrow night we'll take out the east and south roads.'

'Unless you get the information, then that won't be necessary.'

Duh. 'That's correct, sir.'

'I hate to ask, but any casualties? Bearing in mind that our leader said he doesn't want any of this coming back on him.'

Hooper paused for a moment. 'The murder I told you about earlier? We found out today that it was a woman connected to the war memorial committee.'

'Bugger. Make sure you keep well away.'

Silence while Skipper puffed on his pipe. Hooper thought that maybe Skipper should up the ante and start smoking crack. Maybe that would take the edge off.

'Not good, Hooper. Not good at all. The leader will want a sitrep, and now I'll have to tell him that there's a casualty.'

'Well, actually...'

'Don't bloody well tell me there's another one.'

'Tonight, we had to deal with somebody who was going to compromise the operation.'

'A local?'

'We assumed so. He came upon us as we were at the second point. I tried to ignore him but he wouldn't go away. Shouting and bawling he was. So Smart took care of him.'

'Is he liable to cause us any further trouble?'

'No, sir. We have him isolated.'

'Good God. Was there no other way?'

'No, sir. We made it look like an accident and the snow is so bad, both vehicles will be covered by tomorrow.'

'Fair enough. Make sure the others in the team are aware of the situation.'

'Will do, sir.'

Skipper disconnected the call. It was never the other way round.

'The old man whining again?'

'Of course he was. We're on the ground and we

have to think on our feet.'

'He knows the risks. He's always trying to cover his own arse. Fuck 'im. We do whatever's necessary, and upstairs know that.'

'Damn right. Now get the fucking kettle on. You've got me in the mood for a cuppa now.'

'You lot look like you've lost a pound and found a penny,' Paddy Gibb said as Miller and the others came into the hotel bar. 'Don't tell me you let Miller drive?'

There were a few regulars in, and some guests from the play production.

'Nothing as exciting as that, sir,' Miller said. 'Can we talk outside?'

'Of course we can, son. You remember the good doctor?'

'Of course. Pleased to meet you again, Dr Ross.' Miller smiled at the doctor and they shook hands.

Gibb excused himself from the table and they went out into the TV lounge.

'We searched Graham Gorman's house. There's no sign of him,' Miller said.

'You think he's missing?'

'I'm not sure.'

'The pathologist we spoke to on Facetime with

Eve, reckons Ella Fitzroy was crucified post-mortem. That means in all probability, the job was done by two men.'

'That would make sense.'

'We're going to try and find his son tomorrow. Nick Jones gave us the son's address. And while we're on that subject, I told Jones that we needed him with us on this investigation.'

'You don't think we can cope?' Gibb said.

'Not that at all, but for two other reasons; we could do with somebody on hand to show us around, and Sergeant Brown took it upon himself to have Jones follow us tonight and spy on us.'

Gibb gritted his teeth. 'Did he now? I'll get onto Jeni Bridge in the morning and explain to her, but I want you to go over to the station and relieve Brown of his duties. It's not as if he's helping on this enquiry, so we don't need him. I have the authority to remove him and then I'll send a report to Standards. I will not have some jumped up traffic warden sending somebody to spy on my team. Oh no. Fuck that for a laugh.'

'You're okay with Jones being on the team? He's the one who told me about Brown. The boy wants to transfer up to Edinburgh.'

'Tell him to get it in now and I'll talk to Jeni. He sounds like he'll be a good copper back home.'

'He and his pal both want to transfer. PC Gilbert Morris.'

'Tell them to do it tomorrow.'

'I will. Thanks, sir.'

'Now get your arse over to the station and break the news to Brown. Tell Morris he's now an acting sergeant and he can replace Brown.'

Miller went into the bar and motioned for Watt to come with him. Julie was sitting talking to the doctor.

'Andy, we need to go over to the station to relieve Brown of his duties. You up for it?'

'Up for it? Lead the way.' He looked back into the bar and held up five fingers to Eve Ross. *I'll be back in five.*

'You too, Jones,' Miller said to Nick. 'If you're up for it.'

'I'm more than ready, sir.'

Steffi was walking along the corridor, having just been to the ladies. 'Trying to sneak out without buying a round, sir?' she said, smiling.

'Not exactly. We're going to go over to the station and tell Sergeant Brown he's been suspended.'

'Ooh, can I come?'

'Yes, you can. Let's go now and get it over with so I can get back and get a pint.'

Steffi grabbed her jacket and the four of them

walked the few yards across the deserted, snow-swept road to the station.

Sergeant Hudson was on the desk. He buzzed them through to the back.

'Where's Brown?' he asked the uniform.

'Upstairs.' He glared at Miller, his eyes full of contempt.

Miller started towards the stair door when he heard Hudson speaking again.

'Where do you think you're going?'

When Miller turned, he saw Hudson was directing his question to Nick.

'Upstairs.'

'Who said you could do that?'

'I did,' Miller said. 'So it's none of your business, sergeant.'

'This is my station. People do what I say.' He took a step towards Miller.

'Is that right? Not anymore. For the duration of our investigation, PC Nick Jones has been promoted to acting sergeant, and he will be assisting my team. You got that?'

He didn't wait for an answer but instead lead the others up the stairs.

'About fucking time,' Brown said as they walked into the enquiry room upstairs. 'Did you see what those fuckers were up to?'

'I did,' Nick answered. 'And they decided to come back with me.'

Brown spun round. 'Why you little bastard,' he said.

'Don't be talking to one of my officers like that,' Miller said, but Brown turned and looked at him.

'I was talking to you! Who the fuck do you think you are, come down here, a bunch of ponces from Edinburgh, throwing your weight about?'

'We're your fellow officers,' Steffi said.

'Was I fucking talking to you, darlin'?' he said. He took a step forward, sticking his finger out, about to poke Steffi in the chest when she grabbed his finger, twisted his hand, spun him round, and kicked his feet away from him in one swift movement.

'You sexist bastard. Well, this wee lassie was in the British army, and I've seen things and done things that you can't even imagine. Where we come from, we deal with real criminals, not errant fucking sheep. Do you understand? And if any part of your body comes into contact with mine, ever, I will go fucking toe to toe with you. And just before I cut your fucking balls off, I will look you in the eyes and smile. Do you understand?'

Brown said nothing.

'I said, do you fucking understand?!' Steffi screamed at him.

'Yes, yes, now let my fucking finger go!'

Steffi let it go.

Miller looked at the big uniformed officer lying on the floor. 'Get up! You're a bloody disgrace to the uniform. But I'm here to tell you that you have been suspended, with immediate effect.'

Brown got to his feet. 'What? You have got to be fucking kidding me.'

'Insubordination. Attempted assault on a fellow police officer. That's just for starters. Now give me your warrant card.'

Brown handed it over.

'You are not to set foot in this station until further notice. Officer Nick Jones will be on my team from now on, as acting sergeant. I'll have one of the other PCs act as station sergeant. Now, get out.'

Brown stormed out, muttering under his breath.

'Maybe we can get on with our investigation without that pair of twats getting in our way,' Watt said. 'Good job, Steffi. And I just want to say, if I have offended you in any way since we got here…'

'Shut up, Andy,' she said, smiling at his grin. 'You can buy me a drink.'

'We should tell Hudson the news,' Watt said.

'Somehow, I think he already knows,' Miller said, as they left the room.

SIXTEEN

There were more people in the bar when Miller and the team went back across. Including Stuart Love, surrounded by his sycophants.

Gibb was talking to Eve Ross.

'Look at him,' Watt said, 'no doubt trying to impress her with his war stories.'

'Not as much as lover boy, there,' Miller said.

Love was surrounded by young women who were hanging onto his every word. Then he looked over at Miller and excused himself from the small crowd.

'Inspector, I hope you don't mind me cornering you on your night off, but could I ask you for an update? Any progress?'

'This is our first day, Mr Love, so it's early days. We are making progress though, and we'll be sure to keep you in the loop.'

'Thank you.'

'Is your girlfriend holding up?' Watt asked.

'She's distraught. She's back home.' Love walked away.

'I can see how distraught *he* is,' Watt said, as Love went back over to the women who were fawning over him.

'How did it go with Brown?' Gibb said, coming across to them with a glass of whisky in his hand.

'He's pissed off, that's for sure. He didn't take it well, but he left the station after I took his warrant card.'

'What about Hudson? How did he take it?'

'He didn't have an opinion. He's a lot quieter than Brown.'

'Good. We'll start by talking to Gorman's son in the morning, see if he knows anything. Maybe his father took off or something.'

'Right. I'm going back to the hotel,' Miller said.

'I wish you would stop calling it that,' Watt said. 'I wouldn't board my dog there.'

Steffi stepped a little closer to Gibb. 'I want to thank you, sir, for letting me have your room and you move into the boarding house.'

'I didn't say that, did I?'

'Oh, you didn't? I must have misheard you.'

'Watt's smartarseness has rubbed off onto you, Sergeant Walker.'

'Message received and understood.' She smiled at Gibb.

'You know, if it wasn't for my bad back, you could have had the room,' he said. 'Oh well. Bright and early. Nine o'clock in the station after you've had your bacon and eggs.'

He sat back down and left Miller, Watt, and Steffi standing.

'It's either stay here and get pished with Gibb or else back to the boarding hovel,' Watt said.

'I'm sure Paddy would love it if you picked up his bar tab,' Miller suggested.

'Christ, you're right. Sod him.'

The three detectives turned and headed for the exit.

'You lot heading off to the boarding house?' they heard a voice say from behind them.

Watt turned. It was Eve Ross. 'Yes, we are,' he said. 'Or, as it's otherwise known round these parts, *party central*.'

'You don't mind if I walk along with you, do you? I'm staying there.'

'By choice?' Watt said.

'It was cheaper. And it suits my needs. I'm looking to rent a place and the real estate agent says there are several that are about to come onto the market. Until then, party central it is.'

'Well, just you join the club,' Watt said and held the door for Miller and Steffi.

There was a lull in the snowfall but the air was freezing. They all pulled hats on.

'You ever fancy going to work in warmer climes, I hear Siberia is good this time of year,' Watt said.

'That's where this snow is coming from, Andy,' Steffi said, holding onto Miller's arm. Although the snow had stopped, more than a foot was lying on the pavement.

'I know that, Detective Walker.'

Eve laughed as they crossed the road and walked along the pavement towards the boarding house.

'It's not always like this, apparently,' Eve said.

'How long have you been here?' Watt asked as the other two detectives walked on ahead.

'A couple of months or so.'

'Really? Where were you working before this?'

'Dumfries. I just wanted a slower pace of life.'

'Mission accomplished. Until there was a woman brutally murdered.'

'That did bring the pace up a bit.' She held onto Watt's arm as they trudged through the snow. 'Tell me a bit about yourself, Andy.'

'Nothing much to tell. Nothing exciting anyway.'

'Just give me a peek into the world of Andy Watt. You must have some stories, working up in Edinburgh.'

'I was saving them for my memoir.'

Eve laughed. 'You're such a tease, Andy Watt. But let me ask you; are you married?'

The question took Watt by surprise for a moment. It was something that maybe a woman would ask a man in a singles club. 'No.'

'I was just curious. I was wondering if your wife would be jealous that you're being a knight in shining armour, helping a doctor along the road so she doesn't go skidding down on her bum.'

'I've been divorced for a long time.'

They all crossed the lane and Miller took out the key he'd been given. 'Home sweet home.'

'I hope Bunty didn't keep our dinner warm,' Watt said.

'I'm sure it will be in the dog by now,' Steffi said as they stepped over the threshold.

'I'll bet the dog wouldn't even eat her muck,' he started to reply, but then they saw Bunty behind the reception desk.

'Please wipe your feet,' she said to them. Steffi giggled.

'I hope you're not drunk, young lady.'

'I can assure you nobody's drunk, Bunty,' Eve said, stepping forward.

'Oh, doctor. That's okay then. Would you like a cup of tea?'

'No thank you. I have some reports to write so I'll head straight up to my room.'

'Very well.'

They all went up the stairs, Miller and Steffi to the front. Watt and Eve to the back.

'Goodnight, boss,' Watt said.

'See you all in the morning.' Miller went up the other set of stairs behind Steffi.

'I have a bottle of Macallan,' Eve said to Andy. 'And two glasses.'

'Just for medicinal purposes?'

'Sure. If that's what you want to call it.'

'It does. And two glasses, eh? That's very civilised.'

'I don't have many visitors, so maybe yours will have a wee bit stoor in it. Don't worry, I'll rinse it first.'

She got the bottle and glasses from her room, and Watt was waiting for her in his own bedroom. 'Old Bunty would have to change her drawers if she knew I was going into a man's room.'

'And a bad man at that.'

She laughed as she closed the door.

It was in the wee hours when Eve Ross had to go to the bathroom. She didn't like the idea of creeping about in the dark but it was a necessity. Andy Watt was still in bed, snoring his head off.

There was a little night light plugged into a wall socket, just enough light so you wouldn't break your neck tripping over one of Bunty's cats.

She eased down the short flight of steps and was about to go into the bathroom when she saw another bedroom door open.

It was the young female detective. Steffi Walker. Coming out of Frank Miller's bedroom.

Interesting she thought, as Steffi went next door into her own bedroom.

SEVENTEEN

'I don't eat the breakfast here,' Eve said, towelling her hair before using the blow dryer.

'Where do you normally eat breakfast?' Andy Watt said, walking naked across the room towards the chair where he'd thrown his clothes in the early hours of the morning.

'I grab a roll from Gorman's bakery next door. He does filled rolls first thing in the morning. Bacon, egg, and cheese. I know they're probably clogging up my arteries now but they are so good.'

'Gorman? Is that Graham Gorman's bakery?'

'It is. Why?'

'We've been trying to get a hold of him.'

'His son opens the bakery these days. The old man takes over the late shift.'

'I'll talk to him after I shower. Then we'll nip down

for a roll. No doubt my superior officer will be indulging in the heart attack special along the road.'

'Lucky him. He doesn't have to clog his arteries with Bunty's porridge oats. You could hang wallpaper with it.'

'I need to go and shower.'

'Not dressed like that, I hope.' She laughed.

'No, I wouldn't want old Bunty to have a coronary, seeing me in the buff.' He pulled on boxers, trousers and a sweatshirt before going along to the shower with his towel and toiletries. Twenty minutes later, he was shaved and washed and came back to the room to get dressed.

Eve was gone.

He got dressed and went along to Miller's room and knocked.

'Just up, Andy? I've already been out for a jog along by the river and hit the gym. And I did a few laps in the indoor heated pool.'

'Did you bang your head, boss?'

'Oh wait; that was another hotel I stayed in. Did you sleep okay?'

'Off and on. You?'

'Same.'

Miller grabbed his coat and they went to Steffi's door.

'Coming,' she said, pulling on her coat.

They walked downstairs, Watt glancing at Eve's door. He felt a pang of disappointment. He understood that she couldn't be seen coming out of his room, but it would have been nice if she had been in his room after he'd showered. 'Gorman's son works in the bakery next door,' he said, forcing his mind off the subject.

'I'll go and have a word with him,' said Miller. 'Steffi, you can come with me. Andy, can you go along to the hotel and see that Gibb knows how to start Facetime for our meeting with Edinburgh?'

'Sure, boss,' said Watt, disappointed that he wouldn't see Eve at the bakery.

They stepped out into the blizzard. The snow was being driven by a strong wind, taking the visibility down to what seemed like two feet.

They stepped out on to the treacherous pavement. Miller and Steffi turned right and crossed the lane and walked next door to the bakery, while Watt pulled up the collar of his coat and trudged along the pavement towards the Eskdale Hotel.

Miller stepped into the bakery and Steffi closed the door behind her.

'You look like you could do with a hot roll,' the woman behind the counter said.

Miller showed her his warrant card. 'I'd like to speak with Jesse Gorman.'

'Oh, right. You must be one of the policemen from Edinburgh.'

'And women,' Steffi said, holding out her warrant card. The old woman's smile fell away.

'Aye, well.' She turned and went through to the back. 'I'm sure there's a typewriter that's missing a secretary,' they heard her mumble as she disappeared out of sight.

'How many words-per-minute do you do?' Miller said to Steffi, laughing.

'She was meaning you, sir.'

'I knew that.'

'Aye, what can I do for you two police officers?' Jesse said, coming through to the shop.

'We'd like a word about your father. In private,' Miller said as he spotted the old woman hovering behind the baker.

'Sure. Let's go through to the back.'

The two detectives followed him. It was warm and smelled fantastic.

'What's my father done this time?' Jesse asked as they went into a small office.

'We're not sure. We'd like to talk to him but he wasn't at home last night. Have you any idea where he might be?'

'Dad? No. He should have been at home. If he was going out somewhere, he would have told me.'

'Does he tell you every time he goes somewhere?' Steffi asked.

'Oh aye. In case he ends up getting pished. Then he'll call me up like I'm a fuc—, I mean, an Uber or something.'

'And he didn't call you last night?'

'No. My mate came round, and he stayed over, what with this weather. We had a few drinks, but my dad didn't tell me he was going out.'

Miller looked at Steffi before carrying on. 'Were you aware that he was having a disagreement with Ella Fitzroy over the war memorial?'

Jesse nodded. 'Stupid old goat. I told him not to worry about it. There are names being added and one of them is Hugh Abernethy. For some reason, my dad took umbrage at this. Probably because the two sisters came along after they found Hugh's corpse, and then they thought they ruled the roost.'

'Your dad threatened Ella on Facebook, apparently,' Steffi said.

'Oh, it was nothing. He got pished one night and they went at it, slagging each other off. But my dad wouldn't physically harm the old woman. Certainly not kill her.'

'What about you, Mr Gorman? How did you feel about Mrs Fitzroy?'

'She didn't bother me. Me and my pal go along to

the committee meetings.'

'Did you see your father yesterday?'

'Just when he took over from my shift. He spends the afternoons in the bakery these days, winding down until he takes early retirement. God knows what he's going to be doing with himself after that. And then we were at the meeting in the church, of course.'

'You haven't heard from him this morning?'

'I don't hear from him any morning.'

'He's not around, Mr Gorman. That's why we were hoping you could help us with that.'

'I told you, I haven't seen my dad since yesterday.'

'Does he have a mobile phone?'

'He does.'

'Try calling him.'

Jesse took his phone out of his pocket and called his father's number. 'No answer.'

'Can you give us his number? We'd like to track him down.'

'So would I, if he's not answering. He might have gone out and got hurt in this weather.'

Steffi jotted the number down.

'Is there anybody you know who might want to harm your father?'

'No. He talks to everybody. It was only Ella he had a problem with.'

'We'll be in touch, Mr Gorman. Meantime, if you

hear from him, please call the station.'

They left the bakery after buying some filled rolls and battled against the howling wind and the driving snow.

'It's getting worse,' Steffi said.

'It's going to keep getting worse before it gets better.'

There was no traffic as they crossed the road and headed for the town hall.

'Listen, Frank, about last night-'

'Nobody needs to know. Not yet. That's just between you and me.'

She smiled at him. 'Thank you.'

He smiled back. 'Don't worry about it.'

They walked into the station and Hudson was behind the desk again. 'Good morning, sir,' he said to Miller.

'Morning.' Miller and Steffi took their coats off and shook them on the big mat, and they stamped the snow off their boots. He looked and saw there was nobody else in the public area.

'DCI Gibb told me that Jones and Morris are now acting sergeants,' Hudson said.

'That's true. With Sergeant Brown being suspended, we needed somebody to cover here and Sergeant Jones will be accompanying us. That's not going to be a problem, is it?'

'Not at all, sir.'

They started walking up the stairs to the upper level. 'I see Hudson's changed his tone.'

'I think he saw how easily you could have some-body replaced.'

They walked along to the incident room. 'Well seeing they don't have many major enquiries down here,' Miller said, taking Steffi's coat and hanging it up.

'Here's the late shift coming in,' Watt said, pouring boiling water into some cups.

'Did you have a lie in this morning?' Gibb said.

'We were interviewing Jesse Gorman, Graham Gorman's son as Andy well knows. He hasn't heard from his father since yesterday.' He took the rolls out of the bag. They were wrapped in silver foil.

'That puts him up a notch on the suspect roster. And since he's still the only one, that's not a good sign for him.'

Watt made the coffees and handed them to Miller and Steffi. 'Just don't tell them I was being mother when we get back to Edinburgh.' They tucked into the rolls. 'It's not true what they say about you, boss. Your wallet isn't super-glued shut after all.'

'Your turn tomorrow, Andy.' He took a bite out of the roll. 'What's the latest on the truck crashing into the bridge? Anybody know?' Miller said.

Gibb sipped at his coffee. 'The bridge is knackered.

The fire brigade had to let it burn. They put water on it of course, but only after it died down. They could have had more effect if they pissed on it, by all accounts. The truck is going to just lie there until a tow truck can get to it, but God knows when that will be. There's nothing left of the bridge.'

'That's going to be a nightmare when the snow's gone,' Steffi said.

'That's the least of our problems just now,' Gibb said. 'I just called Jeni Bridge and she's wanting a Face-time meeting.'

'Let's not keep the lady waiting then, sir,' Watt said.

They all sat round the large table and then Gibb slid the iPad across to Miller. 'Fire that up, son.'

'I could have done that,' Watt said.

'You stick to working the kettle.'

'What? I'm not a hundred per cent sure, but I think I've just been insulted here.'

'Don't worry about it, Watt. We'll soon have you working the remote TV in your room.'

'You're loving this, eh? TV in your room. And I'll bet you had a nice full Scottish breakfast this morning.'

'I am and I did. To be honest, I think I ate too much.'

When they were all set, Miller hit the call button. When it was answered, they saw Jeni Bridge.

'Good morning,' Gibb said.

'Good morning, DCI Gibb. I have Superintendent Purcell here with me.'

'Good morning,' Purcell said.

The iPad in Edinburgh was positioned so that it showed a good bit of the conference room.

'How's the snow down there?' Purcell asked.

'Bad and getting worse. We're in a valley here, surrounded by hills. It's coming down like there's no tomorrow. How is it there?'

'Bad. The buses were late getting out and it's a restricted service.'

'How is the investigation going so far?' Jeni said. Her voice sounded tinny.

'So far, we have identified one man who we want to talk to,' Miller said. 'He was on the war memorial committee with Ella, but now he's disappeared.'

'Have forensics been to the house?'

'No. This weather is preventing anybody coming from Dumfries. We have limited manpower. We might need a warrant to search his place, but it's doubtful we'd get it.'

Gibb leaned forward. 'I want to talk to you about that in private.'

'That's fine.'

Purcell leaned forward. 'This is not going to be an open and shut case, I take it?'

'No, sir. The snow is hampering us. Plus there was a bad accident yesterday afternoon, involving a petrol tanker. It crashed into the bridge leading into town from the north, knocking it down.'

'Any fatalities?' Jeni asked.

'Just the driver, as far as we know. They haven't recovered the body yet. They only have one fire engine here, and normally they would have called in back-up, but the roads are impassable.'

'Basically, you have no back-up, no forensics, nothing. You're on your own there?' Jeni said.

'That's about the state of it.'

'Okay. Keep me in the loop. I want, at the very least, a daily update.'

'Will do.'

Gibb looked at the team. 'I just want a quick word with the commander then we can move out.'

They filed out of the room.

Watt's phone rang and he excused himself and answered it. A few minutes later, he came back to Miller.

'That was Dr Ross. She wants me to go across and see her.'

'Okay. Take Julie with you. I'll be over shortly.'

Watt and Julie left the station.

EIGHTEEN

The snow was piling up against the side of the buildings in drifts. It was getting thicker underfoot. Some local traffic had moved along High Street, creating tracks, but the rest of the road was impassable.

'I thought last year was bad,' Watt said as they crossed the road.

'Beast number two is going to be remembered for a long time, that's for sure.'

They turned the corner and walked into the hospital car park.

Inside, they shook the snow off their coats.

'I want to live somewhere warm,' Julie said.

'Sounds good to me.'

They found Dr Eve Ross in the refrigeration room, just like the previous evening.

'Sergeant Watt,' she said, smiling at him. 'Thank you for coming over. You too, Sergeant Stott.'

'It's what we're here for,' Watt said.

'I have something to show you.' She had a porter with her and indicated for him to open one of the steel drawers.

When it was open, they could make out a form under the sheet.

'I just wanted to show you a bruise on Ella's forehead. Just under her hairline. It looks like she may have been punched. When you're out looking, you might want to see if somebody has bruised knuckles. It's nothing really, but I just wanted to show you. I'm no detective, mind.'

'I appreciate that,' Watt said. Then to Julie; 'Could you give us a moment, please?'

'Sure.' She left the room with the porter.

'Well, what have you got in mind, Andy Watt? Now that you have me on your own.' She smiled at him and walked up to him, put her arms round his neck and kissed him.

'I was just going to say, I liked us being together last night,' he said when she came up for air.

'Me too. How about having dinner tonight?'

'I'd like that. Your place or mine?'

She laughed and slapped him gently on the arm. 'There are a couple of restaurants in Langholm. One in the hotel, and one in the little hotel across the road from the Eskdale.'

'I don't want to be eating in the same dining room as my boss, so maybe the other restaurant? We can always go to the hotel for a drink if you like.'

'Oh, I think I'd like that very much, Andy.'

There was a knock at the door. Eve stepped back from Watt. 'Come in.'

A nurse walked in. 'Sorry to disturb you, doctor, but we got a call from Mrs Roberts' caregiver. She's not feeling well at all.'

'Thank you. I'll get right over there.'

The nurse retreated and closed the door behind her.

'I'm on-call all the time. One of the drawbacks of working in a small town.'

'It must be hard.'

'It wasn't unexpected. But if you'll excuse me, Andy. I'll call you about dinner?'

'Great. I look forward to it.'

They left the room and Watt caught up with Julie.

'Cosy wee chats with the doctor?'

'It's top secret. I could tell you, but I'd have to kill you afterwards.'

'What time are you meeting her?'

'What?'

'It's obvious she has a thing for you.'

'Away and don't talk pish, Sergeant Stott. I could report you for sexual harassment.'

'So, what time?'

'She's going to call me.'

'Fly old sod.'

'Less of the old.'

By the time they left the hospital, Eve was already gone.

NINETEEN

The team were standing around the log fire in what was once a living room, many moons ago.

Hooper and Smart. And the other two men who Hooper and Smart referred to as Abbott and Costello behind their back. Abbott was their team leader.

'I was on the phone with Skipper this morning and he wants results quickly,' Hooper said.

'Don't we all?' Abbott responded.

'We're getting on with the technical stuff,' Hooper said, 'but these things take time. This snowstorm wasn't forecast when we put this operation into motion, but we're working round it like we always do.'

'We have to forge ahead.'

'I know. We took the north bridge down just as planned. We blocked off the road leading west, putting the boulders across the road. There was a bogey but we dealt with it. There was no way around it.'

'We have the tower to deal with too,' Smart said. 'After that's taken care of, the whole town and surrounding towns will be affected.'

'Are you going to touch the wind farm?'

'We're still waiting for word from London about that. That's going to add another layer if we do that. People won't be happy, and I'm leaning towards just taking out communications. Taking the power would be too dangerous. Same with the landlines. In case a house went on fire or something.'

'We need a quick resolution to this,' Costello said.

'I know that. We're going to ramp it up a bit today.'

'What about the subject's house?'

'Nothing. The police won't find anything either.'

'They're wondering where he is. They think he's guilty of the murder and left town.'

'That just adds another complication.'

'I think we should have a look at the other subject. Somebody has to know something.'

'We can handle that,' Hooper said.

'Good. Get onto that today.'

'Will do.'

'And make sure you take care of any family or friends who might get in the way. Skipper has to realise that we will do what we have to do, or else we'll be upstairs from his office explaining to the department head why this operation is a failure. And I for one, am not willing to risk failing.'

The other three men mumbled agreement.

'Gentlemen, I want a progress report by the end of the day. Meantime, I have to go and see somebody.'

Abbott walked out of the kitchen and felt three pairs of eyes on his back. The three men were trained killers, but he knew that every one of them had respect for him. Because he was a trained killer himself.

TWENTY

'You'll be fine now, Mrs Roberts. Just a little dizzy spell.' Dr Ross smiled at the caregiver. 'Here's a prescription for some new medicine. It will help with the headaches and light-headedness.'

She handed the prescription to the woman and made her way out. She was in the little, dead-end part of Holmwood Drive. There were parking spaces opposite the old woman's house, and Eve carefully made her way across to the car. The snow was thick and falling fast. It was almost like all life was coming to an end.

Which might not be a bad thing.

She swept the thought away as she pulled up the hood on her anorak. *What would Andy say if he found out you were thinking such thoughts?*

Eve pictured his face, his smile, and she could hear his laugh. She was completely captivated by him.

Spending the night with him was just what she needed. It had been a long time since she had spent the night with a man and she had been lucky finding Andy.

She walked down the steps to the Land Rover. God, she hated this big car. Yes, it was a necessity and did its job perfectly, but it was too big for her. Nevertheless, she needed it to get around.

It was one of the long-wheelbase models. She liked the shorter ones, but this big car could double as an ambulance if need be. The regular ambulances were having a hard time getting through the snow. She had told the salesman that she wanted one of the smaller ones, but since she was the new doctor, he'd given her a good price.

She took the broom out of the back and swept most of the snow off the front so she could see out. Then she sat in the driving seat and started the big machine up. The wipers battled the elements, and the heater was starting to kick some heat out again.

She took her phone out and sent a text to Andy. *Looking forward to dinner!*

She sat with her phone in her lap, waiting for a reply. She had to wait a few minutes.

Me too! He replied to her.

She smiled and stared straight ahead. Maybe this was the turning point in her life, the direction she had been looking for. Andy was quite a catch. He was the sort of man a woman could spend her whole life chasing, and then suddenly, he came waltzing into her hospital. She smiled at the thought of seeing him for the first time. She had been like a school girl.

'Doc! Doc!' A hand battered at the driver's window. For fuck's sake.

'What the hell is it? Don't you know you shouldn't fucking well creep up on people like that!'

The man stood in the falling snow. Staring at her. She recognised him. Some idiot from the bar.

'There's been an accident.'

She let out a sigh. 'Is that all? I thought the ambulance was on fire. And you shouldn't creep up on somebody like that. Ever.' She said the last bit with her teeth gritted.

'Sorry, like, but when I saw the Land Rover, I just thought you could maybe come help.'

'Where's the accident?' she said, composing herself. Her hand had instinctively shot to her pocket where she kept the flick knife. Highly illegal. Highly effective.

'Up the road. There's been some kind of traffic accident between a Land Rover and a big digger thing.'

'Did you call treble nine?'

'Aye.'

Just then, her phone rang. It was the emergency

services operator. One of the ambulances was stuck and since she was out in the Land Rover, could she attend while they got another four-by-four?

She told them she could. She was close to the scene anyway.

She didn't remember the man's name, the one who had knocked on her door. 'I'll follow you.'

He ran back to his pickup truck, one of those Japanese things. They would run forever and a day, but she didn't like the look of them. She pulled out of the space and turned left onto the B709. A quarter of a mile later, the pickup stopped and Eve pulled in behind it.

'There's three big fucking boulders over there,' he said, and Eve was sure his face would have gone red if it wasn't red already. 'Sorry. But there are boulders there. Blocking the road.'

She saw them, just white humps in the road. Telephone wires were down and the guardrail was gone in parts.

'Where's the accident?'

'Down the embankment. The Land Rover and the big JCB thing.'

Eve walked over and had a look down the embankment. Trees had been pushed over, revealing the two, burnt-out vehicles, now covered in snow.

'Can you go down and see if anybody needs help?' the man said.

Watch me. 'That will be a job for the fire brigade. It's too dangerous for us. Besides, that didn't just happen.'

The fire brigade would arrive. Eventually. She made a call, telling the operator that the firefighters shouldn't break their necks getting there. If anybody had been alive when the vehicles went over, they weren't now.

TWENTY-ONE

'Where is this joker?' Paddy Gibb said, lighting up another cigarette. He stared up at the church, trying to remember the last time he'd set foot in one.

'I'm sure the minister is a busy man,' Miller said.

'Andy Watt better be a busy man.'

'He's been on a door-to-door before.'

'But not with the country boys. I wonder when the last time was they were on a door-to-door? Selling poppies, maybe.'

'We have to work with what we've got, Paddy.'

'My ex-wife used to say that to me, too.' Gibb blew the smoke around the big Land Rover. 'Here's the useless article now.'

'Not a religious man, then?'

'I used to go every Sunday when me mother – God rest her soul – used to drag me and me brother. Not now though. What about you, son? You believe in a higher power?'

'There has to be something to hold on to when it's time to go, don't you think?'

'A lot of people don't. And that's their choice obviously, but I don't get into arguments over religion or politics.' He stubbed the cigarette out and put it back into the packet. *It's only a stay of execution, you little bastard.*

He opened the door and they stepped out into the driving snow. 'Fuck me.'

'I'll get the kettle on,' Michael Monro shouted to them as they ran as best they could through the deep snow.

'It must be a great job, drinking tea all day with a bunch of old fannies,' Watt said.

'You're a bit sceptical, aren't you, Paddy? And why are you in such a bad mood?'

They walked through the thick snow of the church's car park.

'It's this place. I'm not built for small town living. I've never understood why people would live here and I can't even imagine being born here.'

'Nothing to do with missing Maggie?'

'Oh don't you start. I get enough of it from Watt.'

Miller laughed. 'Nothing wrong with it.' He squinted against the snow just before stepping through the church door. 'It's better than staying in watching the telly on your own on a Saturday night.'

'I do like her a lot. But we're just friends. Watt makes it sound pervy.'

'Do whatever makes you happy, Paddy.'

They walked into the church. 'Everybody takes the piss. I feel like a teenager sneaking about.'

'There are no rules about being friends with a colleague. If that was the case, the police club would be empty.'

'You know what? Sometimes you don't talk pish.'

'Coming from you, that's a compliment.'

The minister was waving at them from the back of the church. 'Kettle's on!' he shouted, his voice echoing through the building.

They walked down the aisle.

'Cherish your little girls, Frank. Before long, you'll be walking them down an aisle just like this one.'

'I know.'

'And trust me, when you get older, it isn't an old wives' tale that each year goes by faster.'

'That's why we have to enjoy this life while we're here.'

'Listen to us, Frank. Getting bloody morose.'

'You'll have me smoking in a minute.'

'There are worse things than smoking. I might test

the waters and see if Monro would object to me lighting up with my cuppa.'

They went through into the hall where the war memorial stuff was set up.

'Oh boy, it seems as if this snow is here to stay,' Monro said. 'I've never seen anything like it. It's almost as if I'm being tested.' He poured the teas and handed out the cups.

'How long have you worked here?' Gibb asked.

'A couple of months. I was sent here to take the helm after the accident.'

'What accident?' Miller said.

'The previous minister was knocked down and killed in a hit and run. They still don't have the driver, but they reckon it wasn't anybody from round here. Word spreads like wildfire, so they would soon know if it's a local.'

'Where was he killed?'

'Just outside. Near the footbridge. Now, it's not for me to judge, but I have heard word that the previous minister liked a drink. There was alcohol in his system, but he had just left the church when he was hit.'

'Were there any witnesses?'

'No. Nobody saw a thing. Poor man.'

'Now that you're here, I'd like to look at the Hugh Abernethy memorial things you and the committee are working on.'

'Of course. Help yourself.'

'Do you think you could run through the Hugh Abernethy story for me again?' Miller said.

'Yes, no problem. If you come over here.' They walked over to a noticeboard on one wall where Monro pointed to some newspaper clippings. 'Hugh was in Iceland, an agent for SOE. A plane was sent from Kaladames airfield in the south to Melgerdi airfield in the north. Now, Iceland was a stepping stone for American planes that were on their way to England. They would stop there to refuel. Hugh was supposed to be on a flight from Iceland to England, on one of the American planes. It should have headed out over the Atlantic. Instead, it seems it was headed back to Kaladames. With another American airman on board, a man who had been recuperating on the hospital ship moored at Akureyri, just north of the Melgerdi airfield.'

'Why was the plane heading south instead of east?'

'Nobody has any idea. The weather was fine for flying over the Atlantic. There was no communication from the American pilots regarding their decision. We'll never know now. They hit some heavy clouds and crashed into the glacier.'

'And nobody saw them until now?' Miller said.

'Not quite. A small group of men went to the crash site where they saw the bodies and the wreckage, but the weather was so bad, they were in mortal danger.

They left, and soon after, the wreckage was covered in snow and ice and disappeared from view. Until two months ago.'

'And there were rumours of him being a traitor, you said.'

'Yes, indeed. Now we know he was on some secret flight. That's why nobody knew where he was.'

'Is it going to cost a lot to erect the new memorial?'

'Quite a bit, but we're getting businesses involved and we're almost there for the total. It's going to be quite spectacular. It will include those men and women who died in the war on terror, who came from the surrounding towns. There will also be room on the memorial for future names. It will be like the Vietnam Wall in Washington, in America.'

Gibb was standing looking at the newspaper articles. 'Did Graham Gorman have any friends on the committee?'

'No. He was a loner. The only person he's close to is his son, Jesse. He knew the sisters of course, but not as friends. Graham owns the town's bakery, but he wasn't a man for making new friends. He played dominoes at the British Legion on a Saturday night, but he didn't have anybody that he would call his best friend, that I know of.'

'Why was he on the committee?'

'The church had asked for volunteers. Graham

came along and he talked his son into helping and a few others gave their time as well.'

Gibb had no more questions.

'If you gentlemen will excuse me, I still have to call some of my parishioners, to make sure they're okay. Give me a shout if you need any more information.'

'We will,' Miller said. Monro left the room.

'If there's any connection to Ella Fitzroy's murder and this memorial, I'm not seeing it,' Gibb said.

'If there's nothing there, then we're back to looking for Graham Gorman. He's the prime suspect just now.'

'And he's skipped off. I think we should go back and have a look at his house. Let the others know where we're going, Frank.'

After they let the minister know they were leaving, they went back to the car.

TWENTY-TWO

The fire engine's blue lights flashed through the snow, which had eased up for the moment.

One firefighter had gone down a ladder which was attached to some ropes. He had carefully examined each vehicle and confirmed that there were no bodies inside.

One of the uniforms from the station was watching nearby, just like Eve Ross was. Waiting to be called over, but Eve didn't think she was going to be needed, and she was right.

'There's nobody in either vehicle and because of the heavy snow, there's no sign of anybody outside either vehicle.'

'Doesn't mean to say they couldn't have crawled away.'

'Unlikely, but not impossible. I'm making a call though; I'm not putting the men at unnecessary risk.'

'That's fine by me. I agree with you; even if somebody did make it out alive, they wouldn't have survived in this cold and snow. Did you get the plate numbers?'

'We're still working on that.'

'If I'm not needed here, I have patients to attend to. But let me ask you something; why do you think there are boulders across the road?'

'I have no idea. If there were to be any road closures, the emergency services are the first to be told, for obvious reasons.'

Eve shook her head. 'Thanks. I'll see you around.'

'Okay, doc.'

Eve walked through the deep snow to her Land Rover, thinking, *if there is nobody in those vehicles, where are the drivers? And why haven't they reported the accident?* She climbed in behind the wheel and started shaking. *It's just the cold, you silly bitch* she told herself. But she sat in the vehicle, telling herself that she would move off when the heat kicked in. She looked out of the window and saw the fire commander looking over at her. She took her mobile phone out and pretended to speak into it. The reason she wasn't moving the car.

Not the real reason.

She reached into her pocket and gripped the pill bottle. Then looked at the clock in the car. She had gone three hours. She was supposed to have taken it with breakfast and when she went back along to her room, she had thought about taking it, but she had been so happy with Andy, she didn't want to spoil things.

Listen to you! You're talking like a druggie whore now! She smiled, hoping the commander wasn't watching her. She felt like laughing out loud. Rolling the window down and just yelling in the air. She didn't need the meds anymore. None of them. They were a crutch anyway, weren't they? That's what she told herself. *Something to get yourself through the day.*

Well, now she didn't need the crutch. She knew full well that some people needed those types of meds, just to help them get out of bed in the morning, and it was true that she had a mild case of the blues. But who could blame her? After what had happened to her.

She started the car up. The commander might come across to her, poking his nose into her private thoughts. She drove away, carefully navigating the big car through the snow. God, she hadn't seen weather like this in a long time.

That's when she saw Angel in the back of the car.

'Jesus! What a fright!'

'You happy to see me again, girl?'

'Of course I am!' Angel, her friend, the one only she could see. The one she could talk to anytime. The one who had got her through the bad times before the pills.

'That's good. I missed you too. And you don't need those damned pills.'

'I know. I was just thinking that.'

'You want to be on an even keel with that new fella of yours.'

'You like him then?'

'If I was real, then you wouldn't have a snowball's chance in hell over me. If you'll pardon the pun.'

She smiled and drove back down Thomas Telford Road, the big, chunky tyres cutting through the white powder with ease. She had a headache coming on, and she knew she should really go back to the hospital, but she wanted to go to the boarding house. She'd already called base and told them she was still out in the field so they wouldn't worry about her. At least it was good to have Angel back.

She made her way into High Street and parked in the little two-car parking bay in front of the Royal Bank. There were no other cars parked in the street in the parking spaces on the opposite side of the street outside the shops. It was almost as if everybody on the planet had disappeared.

She got out of the car and walked across to the

boarding house. Inside, the sound of a TV playing in the TV room met her. Bunty was nowhere to be seen. Thank God. She didn't want to stand and chat.

'You're going to have a look, I hope?'

'A look at what?'

'Maybe that was a poor choice of words. I meant to say, "snoop".'

'You don't mean...?'

'That's exactly what I mean! There's no better way to find out about a man than take the fast track.'

'Oh God, I don't know. What if somebody catches me?'

Angel shrugged. Eve saw she was smoking again. *'What do I know, Eve? It's what I would do. Whatever.'*

Eve looked at her imaginary friend. 'Don't go sulking, now.'

'I'm not sulking. Do what you want. But this way, you could answer your own questions about him.'

Eve could feel her stomach in knots. 'Okay, just a quick look.'

'That's my girl.' Angel blew out a plume of smoke.

'I wish you'd cut that habit out.'

'Don't start that again.'

She walked quietly along to the reception desk and stood in front of it as if she were waiting for Bunty to come and serve her.

Then she stepped round the desk and bent down.

There was a little cupboard underneath. It had a lock on it but Eve had noticed that Bunty didn't bother locking it. She pulled the little door open and looked at the keys hanging on the hooks.

She took one of them and palmed it. When she stood up, she heard Bunty talking in the TV room. She moved quietly, heading for the stairs. In the short time she'd been here, she knew where each step creaked. Coming in late from having got called out to see to a patient, she hadn't wanted to wake anybody up when she came back in, so she knew which step creaked.

Eve made it up to the landing without making a sound. Instead of turning left on the landing, she turned right and went up the short flight of stairs and along the corridor.

She uncurled her hand and held the key to the lock before putting it in. Turned the lock and then gripped the handle. She stood and thought about it. There was no going back if she opened the door and stepped over the threshold.

'Just do it, Eve.'

She turned the handle and opened the door into Andy Watt's room. She quickly closed the door behind her. Stood with her back to the door and she breathed in deeply.

Breathing in Andy's smell. The smell of his aftershave. And if she concentrated hard, she could smell the sex that they had last night.

God, what a wonderful night it was. He had made her laugh, made her feel special and safe. Then they had taken a bottle to his room and they had talked for a while, having a drink and getting to know each other better. Then she had made the first move, kissing him and then slowly stripping him.

Then he had made love to her. Sweet love, holding on to her, making her feel special. And she knew Andy felt exactly the same way as she did. She could just feel it. She knew he loved her. After all, he had made love to her, hadn't he?

'*He must be something special,*' Angel said.

'He is. I love him, Angel.'

She looked around the room, opening the old wardrobe in the corner. Some shirts and jackets were hanging up. She opened the drawers, one by one, running a hand over his clothes. His underwear.

Then she went over and lay down on the bed. It had been made. She lay on the cold duvet, but she still had her jacket on, so she didn't feel it. The cold covers had felt good on her sweat-covered body the night before. She had been lying in this position when Andy was with her.

Eve closed her eyes. She felt alive right now. More alive than she had ever felt.

Then her phone rang. Somebody wanting to Face-time. It was Simon, from Dumfries. Her heart sank when she saw it wasn't Andy.

'How are you going to explain being in his room?'

'Simon, how are you?' she said, smiling at the camera.

'You didn't text me this morning. I was worried.'

'It must be this weather. I think the mobile towers must be getting affected by it.'

'And yet we are having a conversation.'

'Through Wi-Fi. I always thought you were a computer nerd, too. Seems I was wrong.' She laughed.

'How have things been this morning?'

'They're fine.'

Simon was silent for a moment. 'You're not in your own room, are you?'

'No. That detective I had in the mortuary asked me to fetch something for him since I was coming back here anyway. He and some of the other detectives are staying here.'

'You've taken your meds, haven't you? That was the condition you were allowed to go to Langholm.'

'Simon! Listen to yourself. Everything is fine. It's the weather here that's causing havoc. I was called out to a patient first thing, then a road accident. Believe it or not, even though this is a small town, they keep me busy.'

'Glad to hear it. As long as you're keeping your end of the bargain.'

'I told you, I am.' She smiled again. 'And I can't thank you enough.'

'You don't have to thank me, Eve, you just have to work hard at getting better.'

'I've never felt better in my life, Simon.'

'Good. Now, I need to go and cut up a sudden death from last night. Dumfries is busy too.'

The pathologist ended the call.

Eve got up off the bed and looked around once more.

She let herself out of the room quietly. She was about to go to her own room when she heard one of the stairs creak. She waited. It wasn't anybody coming up, it was somebody going down. She eased along the hallway and stopped at the top of the short flight of stairs. When she peeked round, she saw Bunty going down.

The old woman offered a laundry service to her guests. She wondered if the old woman had been listening.

Too bad if she was.

'Push her down the fucking stairs! Nosy old cow!' Angel said. She'd lit up again.

'Indeed I will not.'

Eve went back to her own room. She would go and

hold the packet of razor blades. It had been a long time since she had cut herself, but just knowing the blades were there gave her comfort.

TWENTY-THREE

'That doctor's nice, isn't she?' Miller said as Watt guided the Land Rover over the Thomas Telford bridge. The vehicle slipped but Watt caught the movement and corrected it.

'See? That's how you drive, Miller,' Gibb said from the back seat. 'It's rubbing off.'

Miller made a face and shook his face. 'Anyway, Andy, are you seeing her again?'

'Considering this town is slap bang in the middle of nowhere, and there are only a couple of bars, then it would be safe to say we might bump into each other again.'

Gibb blew smoke out into the car. 'Bollocks. What do you say to that, Frank?'

'Bollocks.'

'There's the bar in my fine hotel for a start. Then

there's one in the Douglas, the Crown, then there's that wee hotel opposite your gaff. There's the golf club and the British Legion. Plenty of watering holes in Langholm. Spill the beans about last night.'

'Look at you,' Watt said, turning into Henry Street at the old police station, 'like a pair of old sweetie wives. I am not the sort of man who would kiss and tell anyway. Dr Ross is a very nice woman, and we had a drink as professional colleagues.'

'Pish,' Gibb said. 'Listening to you talk is like watching a programme you've recorded; you have to fast forward through the adverts just to get to the good bits. We'll be at this old bloke's house shortly, so get to the good bits fast.'

'I never thought, in my career as a highly decorated police officer, that I would one day be stuck in a vehicle with a couple of senior officers who were as depraved as you two.'

Miller looked at him. 'He's right, Andy; if you don't tell us, we'll just assume and then fill in the blanks for ourselves.'

'Christ, it was more fun when we were poking fun at Paddy.'

'Hey, I've told you already, we're just friends.'

Watt laughed. 'See? I just filled in the blanks there, Paddy.'

'Well, if it's just two people having an innocent drink, we'll see tonight, won't we?'

'Don't try and take the heat off yourself by trying to make something out of nothing. I had a few drinks with the doc, and four of us walked back to the boarding house. Isn't that right, Frank?'

'I hate to say it, but that appears to be what happened.'

'You haven't known Watt as long as I have,' said Gibb and blew more smoke into the car as they turned right and headed up towards Graham Gorman's house.

The snow had started falling again. Trees looked like they had never been green and would ever be green again. The wind was blowing the snow so that it was piling up against cars and houses and everything else that got in the way.

'Jesus. Why would anybody choose to live here?' Gibb said again as they passed an empty playground that once held shiny new equipment but was now empty of any equipment at all. Instead, it was used to park highway maintenance vehicles.

Miller saw a JCB backhoe parked up, covered in snow. They reached the unnamed road and turned right onto it, the Land Rover biting into the deep snow.

'No fresh tracks,' Miller said.

'I'll bet the fucker skipped off after topping Ella

Fitzroy. Him and whatever deviant he was with,' Watt said.

'This is a tricky one alright,' Gibb said. 'Nothing turned up from the door-to-door. Nobody in the street across from the church heard anything. And now the minister bloke says old Gorman didn't have any friends. This time, I want to turn his house upside down.'

Up at the top of the hill, the private road veered left. The field below the hill was covered in deep snow and being covered by even more. At its edge ran Wauchope Water, a little river.

They pulled up in front of the house. Nothing looked any different since Miller had been there the day before. They got out and trudged through the snow to the front door. Knocked and waited but got no answer. Then they went round to the back and entered through the kitchen, each of them pulling on nitrile gloves.

Gibb took out a copy of the warrant that had been sent through and left it on the sideboard.

They methodically searched through the house. Going through drawers, cupboards, looking for anything that might implicate Gorman in the murder of Ella Fitzroy.

'Not a fucking thing,' Gibb said.

'Maybe it was a crime of passion,' Miller said.

'Maybe Gorman fancied Ella and tried it on and when she rebuked him, he killed her.'

'What about the other bloke? The person who allegedly helped him?' Watt said.

'Maybe it was his son. Maybe Gorman called him and asked him to help cover it up.'

'Funny way of covering it up,' Gibb said, 'nailing her to a fucking tree.'

'Have you requested his phone records?' Miller said.

'Julie's working on it now, but they're not just handing them over. A warrant was issued and we're waiting now. Records as well as seeing where his mobile phone is.'

Miller took his phone out and looked at the piece of paper that Jesse Gorman had given him. Graham Gorman's phone number. He dialled it and then they all heard it. The phone ringing.

They walked through to the lobby where a linen cupboard was. Miller opened it and the ringing got louder. He rifled through some towels and found the phone.

'Clever bastard. Hiding his phone,' Gibb said. 'Check through it and see the numbers he called.'

Miller started scrolling and saw it was mostly the other number he had scrawled on the piece of paper. His son's phone number. There were several others.

Including Ella's. And her sister. And some other names, all listed with the word *committee* as a prefix.

Miller asked Watt to do a Google search for some of the other numbers. The first one was the bar in the Buck Hotel. The second one was the Chinese take-away in the High Street next to the Buck Hotel.

The third one didn't come up on Google so Miller used his own phone to dial the number.

It went to voicemail so Miller left a message asking the caller to call him back as soon as.

'That's interesting,' he said, hanging up. 'That was Eve Ross's number.'

'The doctor?' Watt said.

'No, the other Eve Ross,' Gibb said.

'You just can't help yourself, eh? If in doubt, use sarcasm.'

'You make it too easy, Andy.' Then to Miller: 'I wonder why the old bloke has Eve's number?'

'She's a doctor,' Gibb said. 'People get ill.'

They left the house. Now they were back at square one, with a killer on the loose.

TWENTY-FOUR

Dan Brown sat in his armchair, stewing. Who did those fuckers from Edinburgh think they were, coming into *his* station and suspending him? Bastards. In his younger days – his army days – he would have taken his frustrations out on some younger squaddie. Or got into a fight with some yokel fuck in a bar. He would go in looking for trouble, and there was always one little scrote who thought it would be fun to knock the big guy down. He had broken more jaws than he cared to remember.

He took another swig of the whisky, thinking maybe he should just arse the whole bottle, but no, he didn't want to go out in this weather half-jaked.

He laughed to himself. They would all eat their words when he was finished with them. He would make them beg to take him back. But he had to prove them wrong first. And that was going to be easy.

Brown lived alone, in a house at the end of a row of houses in Kirk Wynd, a lane off High Street, a stone's throw from the police station. He got up out of the chair and looked out of the window. The snow was coming down hard again.

The daylight was all but gone. Brown had spent most of the day in bed. There was nothing to get up for now. His wife had left him years ago, for a truck driver who was based in Birmingham. He had worked all the hours he could and she had wanted for nothing, but in order to give her the things she wanted, he took extra shifts, and because of the extra shifts, he wasn't around a lot of the time.

She had met this guy online. They had been chatting for several months and had planned her escape like she was doing a life sentence. Which, he supposed, she *was* doing, in her eyes. One day, the truck driver drove up in his car and stopped at the supermarket. Brown's wife popped out for some bread and milk and never came back.

Brown had thought she had gone missing and was worried. One of his officers spotted her car in the car park of the supermarket, but no trace of her was found.

Then he got the phone call later that night. She told him she had left him and had taken everything that she needed. Brown was furious at first but then thought that she wasn't worth it.

The house was rented, and they split everything else and he had never seen her again. Now, Brown suited himself, did what he wanted to do whenever he wanted to do it. And now, thanks to those mutants from Edinburgh, he could do nothing all day if he wanted. Until the federation rep could kick their arses. That wasn't going to happen while the weather was buggering the traffic.

He grabbed a jacket and put it on as he went downstairs to the garage. Being built sideways on a hill, there was a spare room on the ground floor with all the other rooms on the upper level. There was also a built-in garage.

Brown went in there, and into the Subaru Outback that was his. He had given Jones a hard time about his own Subaru, but the truth was, they were great in this kind of weather, and he drove Land Rovers at work, so he wasn't going to own one.

The garage door opened and it looked like he was going to drive over the South Pole. In reality, he was going to go over to Acting Sergeant Jones's house and give him a piece of his mind. Maybe slap the fucker around. He was another interloper. Coming from God knows where, but more than likely Dumfries, swanning into the station like he had worked there for years.

Well, fuck him too. Brown smiled at the thought of giving the other man a good belting. They could shove their job up their arse. He was going to leave this dump behind when the weather cleared.

He crossed straight ahead into Drove Road and carefully followed the road south. The car was fitted with winter tyres, something that Brown had been going to have removed before he read about the impending storm, and the car handled the snow with ease.

He stopped at the top of the hill, just up from the old church that was now the Julie Dumbarton art gallery, and he sat and watched the building just down a bit and opposite.

It was an old industrial building, made of stone, and like the house he himself rented, it was built sideways on the hill. A set of stairs was at the end closest to him. At the opposite end was a steel sliding door.

One window faced the street but there were no lights on that Brown could see. If Jones wasn't in, he was probably at the station. Bastard. Never mind, he would come back later. Better lay off the whisky though. He wasn't worried about driving around the town with too much drink in him, hell, everybody at the clubs did it. That was the only way they could all get home, what with there only being two taxis in town.

No, he didn't want to get pished and come back because he wanted to see the look on Jones's face and be able to remember it tomorrow morning.

He was about to drive down the hill, to get back to the A7 so he could just go home when he saw the steel door sliding open. A black, short-wheelbase hardtop Land Rover came out. It had blacked-out windows. He didn't know that Jones had a Land Rover as well as a Subaru?

The little bastard was up to no good.

He couldn't see how many were inside the vehicle but never mind. Brown had never shied away from a fight in his life. Maybe he would follow the car and see where Jones was going. He reckoned wherever it was wouldn't be going far in this weather.

As the black car turned left onto the A7, Brown followed. Drove Road was in the southern part of the town. The road was thick with snow, but both vehicles were going through it with ease.

Maybe if Brown had had one less whisky, his mind would have been sharp enough to realise that the driver of the Land Rover would see his Subaru, considering there was no other traffic on the road.

They approached the traffic light to go across Skipper's Bridge. It turned green and they went across slowly. Then the Land Rover turned right, into Cemetery Road. It carried on up, slowly. Brown followed, not wanting to put his headlights on. It was dusk, but the snow kept everything light.

The road twisted round and then back on itself and the black car disappeared round a bend. Brown stopped. What the hell was Jones doing, coming up here? And if he followed, there was a good chance the young sergeant would spot him.

Brown knew there was an old caretaker's cottage at the top, which would hide his approach if he decided to go straight up.

He put the car in gear and carried on up. He rounded the bend at the top but there was no sign of the Land Rover. He inched the car forward, seeing the tracks in the snow. They led away round the old cottage, towards the cemetery itself.

This was the new one. He thought that there would be enough spaces up here for the dead for the next couple of hundred years. He parked out of sight behind the old garage and got out of the car.

The wind was howling so he couldn't hear the sound of the engine from the other car. He moved swiftly after pulling up his hood and walked up to the front door of the cottage. There were no other footprints. It was abandoned but not vandalised.

Was Jones coming up here to meet a woman, somebody who was maybe married, just like his own wife had done? Meet a lover.

He went into the cottage. It was a relief to get out of the wind. Maybe if he went out the back, he would be able to sneak around and see what Jones was up to.

He was walking through to the kitchen when he heard somebody behind him.

A figure wearing a balaclava was pointing a gun at his head.

'I really wish you hadn't come up here, Sergeant Brown.'

TWENTY-FIVE

'What we doing for dinner, boss?' Watt said to Miller as they climbed the stairs to their rooms.

'I was thinking of a steak at The Savoy.'

'I was thinking about a steak, too,' Steffi said. 'But I'm going along to the Eskdale.'

Watt shrugged. 'Sounds like a plan. The food is pretty decent in there, unlike this old boot's fare. I bet even the local dogs don't go scrounging in her bins.'

Steffi laughed. 'I'm just going to freshen up and I'll meet you both downstairs, in say, half an hour?'

'Sounds good,' Miller said. 'I'm going to call home anyway.'

They both went up the staircase to the front of the house while Watt went towards the back. He went into his room and took his coat off.

Then he stopped. Somebody had been in his room. Bunty, snooping around? She did say to leave his laundry in the basket and she would take it to wash.

No, this was different. Something seemed to be out of place. He walked over to his chest of drawers and opened the drawers one by one. Nothing seemed out of the ordinary, although he didn't have an abundance of clothes with him.

Then he saw it; the slight indentation in the middle of his bed. Had he sat down on it earlier? He couldn't remember. Never mind. Nothing was missing that he could see.

He was just about to take his jacket off when there was a light tapping at his door. Probably Lizzie Borden. He strode over to it, an acid quip playing on his lips as he expected to see Bunty standing there, but it was Eve.

He smiled at her and stood back to let her in. 'Hello, stranger,' he said.

'It was only this morning,' she said, putting her arms around his neck and kissing him. He hesitated for a second, then let himself relax.

'Where are you eating dinner?' she asked him, gently pulling away.

'We're all eating along at the Eskdale.'

'Mind if I join you? I sometimes eat there anyway.'

'Not at all.'

They made small talk and Eve left to freshen up. When Andy was ready, he went downstairs to the TV lounge and flicked through some channels, stopping on the news.

'Anything good?' a woman said as she came in and sat down.

'Nothing except the weather. Is there ever any good news?'

'You know the old saying, *If it bleeds, it leads*. Nothing bleeding so they always have the weather to fall back on.'

'This is certainly something else.'

'Are you here with the production?' she asked him.

'I'm sorry?'

'The play? Are you part of the production crew?'

'No, I'm a detective.'

'Oh yes, that poor woman. It has a lot of us rattled. Coming to a small Scottish town and finding there's a killer on the loose. Some of us thought it was a publicity stunt.'

'It's no stunt, believe me.' He looked at her. 'Do you know Stuart Love to talk to?'

'Yes. I'm a make-up artist. I do his make-up.'

'How do you find him?'

The young woman smiled. 'He's a nice guy. Not

like some of those other so-called celebrities. Mutants. Stuart's very friendly. Very outgoing. God knows what he sees in that Nancy one.'

Just then, Eve appeared at the door, followed by Miller and Steffi.

'You ready?' Eve asked, glaring at the younger woman.

'Yes, I'm ready.'

'It's been a long day. I could murder a G&T. How about you?'

'A pint sounds just about right. How about you, boss?'

'We're off duty, so I suppose so.'

As they started along the hallway, Watt suddenly stopped. 'I have to talk to Bunty about something. I'll catch up.'

He walked back to the reception desk and hit the small bell.

Bunty appeared with a smile, but it dropped when she saw it was Watt. 'Yes?'

'I forgot to ask you if the laundry was paid on a daily basis or just added to the bill.'

'Added to the bill. If you leave it in the hamper I can collect it.'

'I think I left a receipt in a shirt pocket. I just wanted to mention that, as my ex-wife used to go nuts if a piece of paper went into the machine and covered everything.'

'Well, if you take it out before I collect it, then it won't be a problem.'

'Didn't you already collect it?'

'No, not yet. I collect it in the evening. And may I remind you that there is to be no women in the room?'

'I don't intend to bring any women into the house.' Which was true. Eve already stayed here so she would be letting herself in.

'See that you don't.'

Watt turned and walked away. Had the old woman heard Eve leaving his room early this morning? Eve had told him that Bunty lived on the ground floor. Maybe the floorboards squeaked a lot.

He found Eve waiting outside. Miller and Steffi had walked on ahead.

'How was your day?' she asked him.

'Routine.'

'Are you getting anywhere with the murder?'

'No.'

Eve grabbed hold of his arm as they walked along the snow-covered pavement. The snow had faltered earlier and had stopped altogether now. There was still no traffic on the main A7 through town. Nothing would be able to pass, even if the snow wasn't there, due to the bridge being down.

They reached the hotel, and Eve didn't let go of Watt's arm until he gently prised her off.

Gibb was already in the bar with Julie. 'There you are,' he said, looking at his watch. 'Let's get through to the dining room. My belly thinks my throat's been cut.'

'I'm sure the way you've been putting the lager away, it won't be in doubt very much longer.'

'I only drink in moderation, sergeant, not as if my life depended on it.'

'You don't mind if the good doctor joins us, do you?'

Gibb looked uncertain for a moment, but he looked at his officers quickly in turn. Silently telling them not to talk shop. 'Not at all. Shall we?' He indicated for her to follow him.

They had booked a couple of tables and had them put together. 'Those artsy fartsy people will be down like a pack of hungry dogs in a minute.'

'The production people?' Watt said. 'Some of them are very nice. Hard working.'

'How would you know?'

'I was talking to one of them. A nice young girl—'

'Does anybody mind if I order first? I'm starving,' Eve said, interrupting.

'Not at all, doctor, go right ahead.'

The server smiled, took their drink and food orders and left them to it.

'That was a horrible thing to happen to that truck driver,' Eve said.

'We'll have a team out there examining the bridge and reconstructing the accident when the weather eases up.'

'It just seems like a strange coincidence.'

'What does?' Miller said.

'Now there are two roads blocked in Langholm.'

'What do you mean?' Gibb said, but they stayed silent as the server brought their drinks.

'Well, I was called out to a road accident today. A big JCB machine and a Land Rover had gone over the side of the road and rolled down an embankment. Both vehicles were burnt out and covered in snow. It seems that there were no victims, but nobody had called anything in. I mean, if you were involved in an accident, wouldn't you call the police?'

'Yes, but not if I was injured,' Steffi said.

'It seems that they got out, both drivers I mean, but then why not call? If they were both injured, what are the chances they both got disorientated and walked away, to fall injured in the river? I mean, it could have happened.'

'You said the road was blocked,' Julie said.

'Yes. Three large boulders have been placed across the road. The fire commander said that they weren't given any notification that a road was going to be blocked off, as they would have to be the first ones to know.'

'Yes, but one was an accident,' Gibb said.

'You're right. But somebody blocked that other road with huge boulders,' Eve said. 'I don't think it's a coincidence.'

TWENTY-SIX

'What are we going to do with him?' Costello said.

'Well, we're not going to chop him into little pieces and put him in the open fire.'

'I know that. I was just wondering what we were going to do with him. Where we'll keep him.' Costello had a disappointed tone in his voice, Abbott realised. Fuck. This was only the second time he'd worked with the man, and not for the first time, he felt a shiver run down his spine. Abbott wasn't afraid of anything, but he was wary of this man he had to work with.

'We can get the others to take him away.'

'Oh. Right.'

Again with the psycho look.

Abbott was glad when he heard the other vehicle pull up outside. Hooper and Smart were here. A few minutes later, the two men walked into the room.

Abbott was envious of the relationship the two ex-military men had.

'Anyway,' Costello continued, 'we have a bit of a problem. The copper who got suspended came here, snooping.'

'What?' Hooper said. 'How did that happen?'

'Due to the fact I left my crystal ball back home, I'm going to say, I don't know.'

'Did you kill him?'

'Not yet,' Costello said. 'If there's another way, we won't have to. Skipper will get upset if there are too many bodies.'

'We'll take care of him later. Where is he now?' asked Hooper.

'Through in the other room. We overpowered him and then gave him a little injection.'

'We'll put him beside the other one.'

'There's no chance of him coming round when we're out?' Hooper looked concerned.

'No, I made sure of it.'

'Let's get started then. We have a lot of work to do. I want the landlines temporarily disabled. Nobody can know what's going on here. We have our satellite radios, so we're fine.'

'Skipper doesn't want that done,' Hooper said.

'Skipper's not here, running the show. I am. Destroy it. I don't want any calls getting out.'

'Whatever you say, boss.'

'Right, you two get on with that. We have to get back.'

Five minutes later, Hooper and Smart were riding the skimobiles out of the detached building at the back of the house.

The machines buzzed as the riders navigated their way up the hill, traversing the snow-covered terrain until they came to their target.

The two men were each wearing a backpack and they stepped off their machines next to the tower. The snow had started coming down heavier and the wind was blowing it sideways. Hooper opened his backpack and took out the charges and the C4. A few minutes later, they rode their machines to a safe distance and set the bomb off. The tower crashed down as the two east-facing legs were blown to smithereens.

They rode the machines back to the fallen giant and then placed much smaller charges through the network of metal dishes and framework.

Once again, they got back on the snowmobiles and rode a safe distance away. Hooper set the charges off and the whole tower blew apart, throwing debris high into the air. Flames licked at the steel as smoke rose up to join the snow.

They rode back to the house. There was still much more work to be done.

TWENTY-SEVEN

'Come on, man, you're not serious?' Jesse took a sip of the whisky. He was easing into it tonight.

'I'm going to fucking do it now,' Pinky said, wired up on some hooligan juice already. He picked up what Jesse was now calling *the wee jobby*, and dialled Mary's number.

'*Hello?*'

'I'm watching you, bitch. You're going to get what that old bastard got. Now I'm after some young meat like you. You're going to fucking die.'

He hung up before Mary could answer.

'That's a bit fucked up,' Jesse said.

Pinky switched the phone off before it could ring. 'Fucked up nothing. She'll be pissing her pants by now. I'm telling you, if they don't want us to protect them now, there's something seriously wrong.'

'There's something fucking seriously wrong with *you*. Jesus!'

Pinky laughed.

'Maybe they won't want to go out now. Maybe they won't go to the play,' Jesse said.

'They will. They're part of the Langholm Actors Group. They're extras in the play.'

'I hope you're right, Pinky.'

'Of course I'm right.'

'I'm going to call Mary now on my own phone, then we can arrange to pick them up and go to the committee meeting.'

'I'm getting bored with this pish. Fucking memorial,' said Jesse.

'That's not very patriotic.'

'Bollocks. You're only there so you can give Mary a bit of spiel.'

'I might just be the head hospital porter –'

'The only hospital porter.'

'But she thinks I want to study online to get a degree to move on.'

Jesse laughed. 'Oh fuck. That would do it right enough. Give her hopes of you buggering off somewhere so she can tag along. What are you going to do when it all goes out the window?'

'It's not as if I'm going to marry her or anything.'

'If her father thinks you're shagging his daughter,

you won't have any choice, my son. I bet the old bastard's polishing his shotgun right now. Besides, Mary's in her late twenties, never been married. She might see you as her last hope.'

'What? Fuck off. I'm a better catch than the mutant she used to go out with.'

'He had a new car.'

'So what?' He dialled Mary's number.

'Who the fuck is this?'

'Oh, hello, Mr Patterson. It's George calling for Mary. Is everything okay?'

'Oh, it's you, son. No, everything is not okay. Some bastard just called and threatened my daughter.'

'Good God. Who was it?' He heard the phone being taken away from Patterson's ear and him speaking, telling somebody who was calling.

'I have no idea. I think it might be that shitehouse who lives in Annan. Well, as soon as the weather clears, I'm going to go down there and boot his cu—'

'Oh George, thank God it's you. My ex keeps calling and threatening me. I'm scared, George.' Mary had taken the phone from her father.

'Don't you worry about that, Mary. I'm at Jesse's house. We can swing by and walk with you and Isabel to the church.'

'We'll be ready in ten.'

'It might take us a bit longer than that since we're walking but we'll be there. See you soon, Mary.'

He was still holding the phone, waiting for her to say goodbye, when he realised his phone had no bars. 'Bastard thing, but at least I got the job done. Didn't I tell you, Jesse?'

'Okay, you win, but if you get caught, I know fuck all about this.'

Pinky laughed. 'I don't think her father will worry about whether we get the jail or not.'

They left Jesse's house in Mary Street and walked over the Thomas Telford bridge. The snow was coming down harder again and they had to duck against the blizzard. The high street offered little relief. It was enough to keep both men from talking as they walked south. It took fifteen minutes to get to Rosevale Street. They walked down the hill to one of the terraced houses on the right.

Mr Patterson answered the door, holding a hammer in his hand. 'It's you, George. Thank God. Come away in. Isabel's here too. Hi, Jesse.'

The men stepped over the threshold. Pinky hoped his face wasn't going red. Was Mary's father looking at him funny? Did he really know it was Pinky who had made the call?

Mary and Isabel were sitting in the front living room. Mary got up. 'Oh, George!' She rushed over to him and threw her arms around him. 'I was so scared. I think the maniac's after me.'

'I'm going to kill the bastard,' her father said. 'I'm going to drive down there and snap his fucking neck.'

'Let the police deal with it,' Mary's mother said.

'Like fuck, I will.'

'You will! For Mary's sake!'

'She's scared out of her wits. We don't know if it's that fucking creep in Annan or this sick bastard who killed poor Ella.'

George gently prised Mary away from himself. 'Let me tell you something; Mary is safe with me. Me and Jesse will look after these two girls. We won't let anybody come near them. We'll stick together and if any scumbag comes near us, he'll get a bloody good hiding.'

George was breathing hard as the others stood and looked at him, not sure if he had any more to say. When it was clear that he didn't, Jesse stepped forward.

'Nobody will come near these girls,' he said. It fell a little flat, but after what Pinky just said, it was acceptable.

Mary's dad stepped forward and put his arms around the shoulders of both men. 'I am bloody proud of you two. Now I feel safe. But if you encounter anything, you call me and let me know.'

'The phones are out now, Dad. Even the mobile phones.'

'So, listen, Dad, after our committee meeting, we were going to go back to Jesse's house for a little drink. I won't be able to call you and we might be a little late.'

'That's fine. As long as these boys can walk you home.'

'We will, sir,' George said.

The girls got their coats on and the four of them walked out into the snow.

TWENTY-EIGHT

Skipper's Bridge was the main bridge at the south end of Langholm, carrying the A7 over the River Esk. Traffic was controlled by a set of traffic lights. Hooper was the electrical genius, so he was the one who opened the traffic-control box at the side of the road, and put the traffic lights on permanent red. There was also a traffic light at the end of an unnamed farm access road. There shouldn't be any traffic, but you never knew. The farmers were hardy bastards round here. None of them drove home from the British Legion without being pished and they threw cows for sport.

'Right, that's it,' he said, going into the brick shed at the bottom of Cemetery Road. 'The phones are out now.' This was where the council workers kept all of their cemetery and grass cutting machinery. 'Let's get this show going.'

'It won't take long. The bigger bridge would have taken longer, but we've blown up bigger shit than this in no time at all,' Smart said.

'Christ, I miss this stuff. I wish we got to play with explosives a lot more.'

'Me too. But just be thankful we get to do it now and again.'

'I haven't killed anybody in a long time, either.'

'For fuck's sake, Hoops, don't get all sentimental on me now. We'll go south of the river when we go home and kick the shit out of half a dozen plebs when we get home. That should tide you over for a bit.'

'Just half a dozen?'

'We'll see how it goes. Meantime, we have a bridge to bring down.'

Smart climbed into the old backhoe and started it up. It was old, but they had fitted a jack-hammer to it. And it had worked perfectly when they had tested it out.

Hooper opened the big sliding door and Smart felt like he was driving down in Antarctica as the wind whipped the driving snow. He turned to face left, then put the machine into reverse. The JCB made mincemeat out of the snow that had piled on the road and he knew if he got stuck, there was a bucket on the front that would bail him out. But he got to the little bridge with no problem.

This bridge was literally right next door to the shed. Drivers wouldn't know it was a bridge if it wasn't for the little wall either side. It carried the road over Nicholson's Sike, a little stream that joined the River Esk on the other side.

Smart stopped and turned the seat around. Then he got to work. The jackhammer ripped down into the tarmac on one side, and soon the wall fell into the stream below. He made sure the machine was on solid road and began to work his way across. Soon, a gap appeared and then the bridge was gone, crashing down into the water below.

He drove the JCB back to the shed and Hooper closed the doors behind him. When he turned the engine off, Smart jumped down. 'That was fun, but not as much fun as blowing the fucking thing up.'

'Come on, let's get back. We've done our part. The others can do theirs.'

TWENTY-NINE

'Welcome!' Michael Monro said.

'Hello, minister,' Mary said.

'Before we start, I would just like us all to take this time to say a prayer for our lost friend, Ella.'

They took their coats off and sat in the chairs around the table and Monro said a prayer for Ella. 'I see we're missing two other members of our group. Jesse, is your father coming along tonight?'

'I haven't heard from my father. He might have gone to see my aunt over in Canonbie. He takes off sometimes.' This was a complete lie. Jesse knew his father was a big drinker, even more so since the death of Jesse's mother, but to tell the minister that his father was away on the lash somewhere, didn't sound as good.

Monro nodded. 'Has anybody seen Ann Fraser?'

Nobody had.

'I'll go along to the house and see if she's coming,' Mary said.

'I'll come with you,' Jesse said, standing up.

'No, it's fine.'

'What if your ex-boyfriend is out there, watching? Or the killer?'

Mary put her coat on. 'Walk me to the door, Jesse.'

When they were at the door of the church, she turned to him. 'Christ, are you soft in the head?' She reached into her handbag and brought out a Stanley knife. 'I only acted upset in front of my folks so I could spend the night with you. Trust me, if any fucker comes near me, I'll slice the bastard.' She smiled, kissed him, and put the knife in her pocket.

'I won't be long,' she said.

Jesse went back inside, dying to tell Pinky that he went to a lot of trouble for nothing. The women were going to come back to the house without them scaring the shit out of them.

Mary walked along the church driveway and into Caroline Street. She kept her hood down. She wasn't one of those stupid twats who thought it was safe to walk about with a hood up or headphones in, so you couldn't hear somebody coming up behind you.

She walked in the middle of the road. She would

hear a car coming. She might not hear somebody coming up behind her, but she didn't want to be grabbed and slammed against a wall.

The thought of Ella being grabbed and taken into the cemetery did put the wind up her, but it didn't scare her. She wasn't scared of anybody. Especially not George *Pinky* Malone. She thought it was him who had called and tried to scare her. She thought there was very little chance it was the killer who had called her. What reason would he have to call her?

And it certainly wasn't her ex-boyfriend, who had taken a court order out against *her*. That was something her mum and dad didn't know about. Her ex was scared shitless of her. He had slapped her one night. Had the fucking audacity to lift his hand to her. Big fucking hard-man. If she had been one of those little weaklings who shrivelled up when a man hit them, then her ex would have been all over her.

But she wasn't.

It had happened in his little flat. In the kitchen. Where there were so many weapons at hand. As soon as the palm of his hand had connected with her cheek, she had turned to the cooker where a twelve-inch frying pan was sitting. She had reached out, grabbed the handle and swung it hard all in one fluid movement.

He hadn't expected that. He had thought she would start crying, promising him anything he wanted. Well, fuck that. She'd put so much force behind the swing that she'd annihilated his nose. He'd screamed as the blood exploded out across the kitchen floor. He'd dropped to his knees and Mary had almost brought the pan down onto the back of his head, but instead, she'd thrown it to the other side of the kitchen and then kicked him hard in the guts, like she was trying to punt a rugby ball over the posts.

Then she had reached down and grabbed his hair and pulled hard, wrapping her fingers in it, bringing his face up until he was looking her in the eye. With her other hand, she had reached up to the kitchen counter and grabbed the kitchen knife that was lying there and turned it so the blunt top of the blade was against his throat.

'I'm going now, and I never want to see you again. But let me tell you one thing, if you ever lift your fucking hand to me again, I will come here when you're sleeping and cut your fucking throat.'

He'd looked at her, tears in his eyes, unable to speak.

'Do you believe me?'

There was a slight nod.

She'd taken the knife away and let go of his hair.

'You cheeky bastard. This is for even thinking about hitting me.' She'd thrown the knife down on the counter, walked behind him while he was still on all fours, and kicked him hard between the legs.

'If you see me coming towards you, anywhere you're at, turn around and walk away. If you get in my face again, I'll open up your carotid with a knife. I carry one everywhere.'

Mary had walked out, leaving her ex crying on the floor. It was shortly after that she got the restraining order through the post. Fuck 'im, she never wanted to see him again anyway.

Pinky didn't know Mary, not really *know* her. She wasn't exactly a hundred per cent sure, but she was convinced he had made the calls, just to frighten her. Mary wasn't frightened of anybody. She was known as a fighter in high school. The first cow that had spoken to her the wrong way had had the living daylights belted out of her.

This was the real reason she was touching thirty and hadn't been married. Her temper. She was a Gemini, and true to the star sign, she had two sides to her. Sweet, fun-loving Mary who liked boys, and the utter psycho, who hated boys. She liked sex, she just didn't like the fucking games people played.

And Pinky calling her up so he could be the tough

man who would protect her took playing games to a whole new level. She would play along with him, simply because this was what *she* wanted. She got to the part of the street where it intersected with Henry Street. She crossed over into Wauchope Place.

In a way, she sort of hoped she would come face to face with the big man who had killed Ella. Some of those serial killers thought they were hard-men. They weren't. They were pond life who blamed their upbringing on turning psycho. She would put him out of his misery.

This fucking snow was really getting on her tits now. Why couldn't it just fuck off so the warm weather could come in? Maybe there was a future for her and Pinky, but it was only a small chance. Would she really want to be married to some twat who made threatening phone calls to a woman just so she would sleep with him? No, he was alright for a bit of fun, but that would be the end of the line for him. She would move out of her parents' house and move to Edinburgh, or maybe down south. Somewhere far away from here.

Ann's house was in darkness. Maybe she'd just gone to bed, feeling the strain of Ella's death. What if she was too scared to walk alone to the church for the meeting? Why didn't that arsehole of a minister think of that? Jesus.

She had to climb over the small gate as the snow was so high everywhere, it couldn't be opened. Nobody had been out shovelling. Anyway, as soon as the snow was removed, it came back down with a vengeance.

Christ, it was freezing. Smoke was coming out of Ann's chimney, so at least she had a fire going. She was about to knock on the door when she noticed it was ajar.

Now that was stupid. She was letting all the cold air in for a start. And that nutter could be anywhere.

She started pushing the door open and then stopped when she heard somebody.

'Tell me where the fucking thing is!' she heard a voice say. It was low but full of menace.

What the hell was going on?

No more time for stealth. If this was the guy, he was going to get his rocks booted right off.

'What the fuck is going on here...?' she said, then stopped. The house was in darkness, the only light coming from the flickering of the flames in the fire-place. Ann was sitting on a chair, a man bent over her. He had grabbed the front of her sweater and he was pulling her face towards his. He let her go when he heard Mary. He stood up and turned to face her.

'You? What the fuck do you think you're doing, you fucking weasel?'

The killer stood and smiled at her. 'Do you want the same as what she's going to get?'

Mary couldn't talk, but she felt the cold steel of the knife in her hand. She was going to slice this bastard.

Before she could take it out, she sensed somebody behind her, and a piece of electrical cord was put over her head and pulled tight round her neck.

THIRTY

Like the previous night, Miller and Watt headed back to the boarding house with Steffi and Eve.

'You fancy having a drink later?' Eve said to Watt after they said goodnight to Miller and Steffi.

'Okay. We can have a drink in my room when everybody else is settled. Just knock on my door and I'll be waiting.'

'I have to go and see a patient first. I want to make sure she's okay. I won't be long.' Eve stood and watched as Watt went upstairs, and instead of going upstairs, she turned and headed back out.

Miller tried calling Kim but his mobile phone had no bars. He tried the landline phone on the bedside cabinet. It was dead. He had lost all communication.

There was a knock on his door. It was Steffi.

'What happened to the phones?' Steffi asked.

'I think the communication with the outside world just died.'

'Do you want me to go?'

He shook his head. 'No. Stay for a while. Grab the bottle and two glasses.'

Steffi poured the whisky and they sat and chatted.

A while later, there was a knock on the door.

Miller got up from the bed and stepped quietly up to it. 'Hello?'

'It's Acting Sergeant Jones, sir. I was just at the station when one of the uniforms came in. There's been another murder.'

Miller unlocked the door and opened it. 'Where about?'

'Down by the footbridge. Actually, the body is hanging from the footbridge. DCI Gibb's there and he sent me along here since the phones are down and none of the radios are working.'

'We'll be right down. I'll get the others. Wait downstairs for us.' He closed the door. 'Time to go back to work.'

The five of them left the guesthouse, Jones leading the way. It was a little after ten o'clock. The snow had slowed down but was adding to the pile that was already there. It was bitterly cold, and Miller couldn't remember what it was like to feel warm outside.

John Street was just along from the boarding

house. It was a narrow street filled with little houses. It led right down to the river and the footbridge.

Sergeant Hudson was sitting inside one of the Land Rovers at the metal barrier at the end of the footbridge, designed to stop cyclists from speeding over. Paddy Gibb was inside the car and got out with the sergeant when he saw his team.

'What's going on, sir?' Miller said.

The end of the bridge had bulbs hanging from it, enough so the end of it was lit up. Several officers were in the middle of the bridge, one of them taking photos.

'There's somebody hanging by their neck from the bridge, in the middle.'

'Do we have an ID?' Watt said. Eve Ross was standing next to him, her medical bag in one hand. She had told him that one of the uniforms had seen her walking back to the boarding house and had stopped her to tell her of the situation.

'Not yet. We haven't pulled them up yet. Whoever it is, is wearing a dark anorak with the hood up, and the rope is pulled tight. I wanted photos taken before they were pulled up. Doctor? Can you go and do the exam, please?'

'Yes, of course.'

They walked onto the footbridge, which was slippery. Miller saw the lights from the church's driveway at the other side. This scene wasn't far from where Ella Fitzroy had been found. He could feel the gentle motion of the bridge as they walked into the middle. There were flashlights shining down onto the body.

'You lot finished taking photos?' Gibb asked.

Miller saw the collar of a pyjama top sticking up from underneath a sweater that Gibb had pulled on. He wondered if Andy Watt knew that Steffi had been in his room. Miller knew that Watt was – if not pleasuring – at least spending time with the good doctor.

The wind whipped down the river. He could hear the harshness of the water rushing below. The streetlights did very little to illuminate the bridge, but another patrol car was at the opposite side of the bridge with a small group of people standing around who were being kept away from the scene.

The blue lights from the cars flashed in the dark.

'Right, get them up.'

The uniforms heaved on the body until the hood first appeared. Miller couldn't see who it was. The body was laid on the snow-covered bridge.

'Cut the rope but well away from the neck,' Gibb instructed. 'We want to preserve the knot.'

The hood had been pulled tight on the head and Miller looked down at the pale face. It looked sort of familiar but he couldn't say if it was a man or a woman.

Eve Ross stepped past him, knelt down, and examined the body. 'I can confirm life extinct,' she said when she was done.

'Do you know who this is?' Gibb said. 'Anybody?'

Eve stood up. 'It's Mary Patterson. A young woman who lives in the town.'

'Go and talk to that group on the other side of the bridge, Frank. I'll get Hudson to take me to her family. I'll be at the hospital if you need me.'

Miller, Watt, and Jones started walking across the bridge to small group huddled together on the other side.

The snow had stopped and the orange glow from the streetlight twinkled on the snow lying on the ground.

'Can you tell me your names, please?' Miller said. Watt was taking notes.

'As you know, I'm Michael Monro,' the minister said. 'This is Jesse Gorman, George Malone, and Isabel Barclay. They're all friends and part of the committee. Can I ask, do you have an identification for the poor soul who was hanging there?'

'Can we talk in the church, please,' Miller said.

'Is it Mary?' Pinky said, his voice rising. 'She went to look for Ann Fraser, along to her house, and she didn't come back. That's why we decided to call it quits. Then when we came out, we saw that person hanging from the bridge.'

'I can't tell you just now. Please go inside.' He turned to Watt. 'Take a couple of uniforms along to Ann Fraser's house. It's the first house on the left in Wauchope Place.'

Watt nodded and jumped into a Land Rover with a uniform and they took off slowly along Caroline Street while the others went into the church.

Inside, the heat felt terrific after the razor-sharp cold.

'Right, tell me what happened. From the beginning.'

Miller and Nick Jones stood at the head of the table while the others sat down, Isabel holding onto Jesse and crying. Suddenly, she stopped and then pointed angrily at Pinky.

'He did it! That bastard! Mary said she thought he had called her, threatening her. He said he was going to kill her!'

'Wait! No, that's not right. It isn't what it looks like.'

'Can I try your phone? There are all sorts of problems with the phones tonight.'

'Go right ahead.'

Miller picked up the handset that was on a sideboard but there was no tone. 'Dead,' he said.

'This weather must be knocking out the phone lines or something,' Monro said.

A few minutes later, Watt came back in, out of breath. 'A word outside, please, sir.'

Miller went out with him. 'What's wrong, Andy?'

'There's no sign of Ann Fraser. Her front door was wide open. There are footprints in the snow on her path, but no sign of her. She must have left, but it's strange she didn't leave her door locked.'

'Christ. Two of the committee members missing and one murdered. That's all we need. Right, let's get this lot over to the station.'

THIRTY-ONE

Sergeant Hudson slowed the Land Rover to a halt outside Mary's house, the big vehicle slipping sideways before coming to a complete stop.

Gibb got out and slipped in the snow and reached a hand out to grab the side of the car, but he went down hard.

'Fuck me,' he said as Hudson came round to help him up. 'Fucking snow.'

'You okay, sir?'

'Lucky the snow is deep. Christ, I can't wait until summer.' Flustered, he wiped the snow off as he walked up to the front door with Hudson.

Mary's father answered after Gibb knocked. 'Mr Patterson?' he said, holding up his ID. The man nodded. 'DCI Gibb, Police Scotland. Can we come in?'

Patterson stood to one side. 'What's wrong? Is it Mary?'

The house had a narrow hallway with a door off to the left. The living room. Mrs Patterson had stood up and was standing in the middle of the room wringing her hands. 'What's wrong? Is it Mary? Has he harmed her?' With each question, her voice rose a little higher.

'Would you please sit down?'

'No, I fucking won't,' Patterson said. 'That's what coppers say when they're going to break bad news.

'If you wouldn't mind, sir.' *My fucking hip is killing me*, Gibb thought.

'Fucking tell us, man.'

And boom, Gibb lit the blue touch paper. 'We found a young woman earlier who was murdered. We believe it could be the body of your daughter, Mary Patterson. We'd like you to come along to the hospital to make an identification.'

'What? Mary. Dead?' Mrs Patterson said. 'Oh my God. What happened?'

'We can't go into exact details yet, but we need you to come along to the hospital.'

The parents shuffled about, getting their coats, grabbing keys, making sure the gas cooker was off. Patterson put a fireguard in front of the burning logs in the fire.

He patted his trousers down before he left, as if he

was making sure his wallet was there, or car keys, even though he wouldn't be driving.

They went outside and got into the police Land Rover.

The Pattersons sat in the back, Mrs Patterson crying throughout the short drive to Thomas Hope.

They were led inside through the falling snow.

The body had been brought back after all the photos had been taken.

Inside the mortuary, one of the refrigerated drawers was opened and the body brought out, covered in a white sheet. The Pattersons were huddled together as Eve Ross gently pulled the sheet back.

'Oh fuck,' Mary's father said when he saw his daughter lying on the steel table. 'That's my Mary.'

Eve pushed the drawer back in.

'I'm sorry for your loss,' Gibb said.

'I only saw her a couple of hours ago. How the fuck can this be happening in Langholm?'

'We'll get to the bottom of it.' Gibb's words sounded more confident than he felt. It had gone from being an isolated murder to some nutter on the loose, killing women.

He turned to Sergeant Hudson. 'Call the station and see if those witnesses are there, giving statements.'

'Will do.' He walked out of the examination room.

'I'll have one of the other officers drive you home,'

Gibb said to the parents. One of the constables ushered them out.

'What a hell of a night,' Gibb said to Eve.

'I can't believe this is happening in Langholm either. When I came here, I thought it was going to be a more relaxing way of life.'

'More murders have happened here than in Edinburgh. And two of the main roads into the town are blocked off. He's still here. We need to find him before he kills again.'

'Three,' one of the other uniforms said, coming into the room in a hurry.

Gibb turned to him. 'What?'

'Three roads, sir. Well, technically two roads and one other. Both ends of the A7 are impassable. We got called out to a road accident. The radios are down but a driver came into the station. The bridge is gone on the A7. They need Doctor Ross there.'

'Skipper's Bridge?'

'No, sir. There's a smaller one past there going south. It goes over a stream that runs under the road.'

'It collapsed under the weight of the snow?'

'No. They were doing roadworks at it. There's a cottage right at the bridge. The occupants saw a JCB doing some work there earlier, and they thought it was emergency roadworks. Then a while later, they heard a crash. A car has gone into the gap in the road and smashed into the river below. The other emergency services have been called.'

'Now three roads are impassable coming into Langholm?' Eve said. 'There are other roads, right?'

'One very tight B road at the side of Skipper's Bridge, the B6318 that leads to a small place called Penton. There's also the B7068, the road to Lockerbie, but it's full of twists and turns. You'd need a bloody tractor to drive along that road, and even then, it would be hard.'

Gibb turned to look at Eve. 'You'd better go. I need to go over to the station and see what's going on with that group. I'll see you later.'

The doctor rushed out with the police officer.

Hudson came back in. 'The radios are out.'

'So I heard.'

THIRTY-TWO

The others were taking statements while Miller and Watt were interviewing Pinky. 'From what we've been told, you didn't leave the church earlier tonight. You have an airtight alibi for when we know Mary was murdered. However, we believe the killer isn't working alone.'

'Aw, wait a fucking minute,' Pinky said, sitting up even more straight. 'I didn't touch her and I don't know who did.'

'Really? Because Jesse is sitting next door telling us you're a pair of killers. That you threatened Mary to get her scared, and then you killed her. Where were you the other night when Ella was murdered? Oh, that's right; you were at the committee meeting. She left early but never made it home.'

'You see the pattern here, George?' Watt said. 'Why don't you just get it off your chest?'

'Fuck off. You're talking shite. I didn't murder anybody.'

Miller slammed his hand down on the table, causing Pinky to jump. 'I think you're the one talking shite, Malone. Are you denying you called Mary and threatened her?'

'I'm not denying that, but that's not how it was.'

'Tell us how it was, then, George,' Watt said, staring at the younger man.

'Fuck me. All I wanted to do was scare her, so me and Jesse could be the heroes. You know, be their protectors. I like Mary a lot. I know it was stupid, but there was no harm meant. And I certainly didn't touch her. Me and Jesse were with that wank Monro all evening.'

Miller raised his eyebrows. 'The minister's a wank now, is he?'

'Of course he is. Do you see him crying over Mary's death? No. He bounds about like he's smoking something. All jolly and happy and everybody's friend. Total wanker.'

'He's a minister. It's his job to keep it together.'

Pinky shrugged.

'He's new, isn't he?' Miller said.

'Aye. The poor bastard that was there before him got himself run over. And I don't suppose the flying squad have solved that one, have they? We might not be the drug capital of the Borders, but there are crimes being committed here and you lot are doing fuck all about it.'

'That's enough,' Miller said. 'We're going to get a search warrant and go through your house. And then when they find out in prison that you're a beast, they'll rip your nuts off.'

'Oh God. Listen, I'm giving you permission to search my house, but the phone you're looking for is at Jesse's house. He lives in Mary Street. The phone is in a kitchen drawer. Go and look at it. You'll see that hers is the only number I've called.'

'Right. We'll do that right now. Andy, come with me.'

They left the interview room and Miller switched off his recorder. 'Send young Nick Jones round to Jesse Gorman's house to look for that phone.'

'You don't think Malone is the killer, do you?'

'No. He and Jesse were in the church with witnesses. But I do want to see that phone. I want you and I to sit down with Gibb. There's something going on in this town.'

'It's weird alright. All the bloody phones are out.'

They went along to their makeshift enquiry room. Nick Jones was there talking with Gibb.

'Sir, sorry to disturb you.'

'No problem, son. What's up? Did that reprobate confess?'

'No, he didn't.'

'Pity.'

'I'd like Jones to go along to Jesse Gorman's house and look for a mobile phone that Malone used to call Mary and scare her. He said it was just a joke, that he only meant to put the wind up her, but I want to see if there are any other numbers on it.'

'Sure.' He turned to Jones. 'Get along there. Get the house keys off Gorman, tell him we need to check something. If he says no, we'll all go round and smell the gas leak so we can kick his fucking door in.'

'Yes, sir.' Jones left the room. A few minutes later, he came back with the house keys. 'He gave me them no problem.'

'Then get a move on. I don't want to let Malone go until we've checked the phone.'

'I'll go there right now, sir. It won't take me long.'

After he left, Miller and Watt sat down at the table. 'What's on your mind, Frank? And I hope it's a suggestion that we all fuck off somewhere warm for a hooly after this.'

'That's the second thing I was going to talk about. The first thing is an idea that came to me.'

'Go on.'

'I got to thinking, this is a close-knit town. Nothing ever happens. But one thing that stuck out, and what we've all seen for ourselves, is that they want to build a new war memorial. That's been the whole key to what's been going on. But it was just a little committee in a one-horse town miles from anywhere, until the body of famous playwright and wartime spy, Hugh Abernethy, was found. That was the turnaround.'

'Okay, where does that leave us, Miller?' Gibb took his cigarettes out and lit up.

'Everybody knows everything in this town. Everything. Each and every one of the people who live here, know what's going on. You could almost see the smoke signals between neighbours. If something is amiss in a town like this, then the people know about it. Agreed?'

'Get on with it, Miller, before my bladder tells me I have to go and exercise it again.' He looked at his watch. 'I should be tucked up in bed by now.'

'Aye, Frank, I'm with Paddy on this. I want to get to my scratcher soon,' Watt said.

'Just get doctor Eve to go ahead and warm it up for you, Andy.'

Gibb looked at Watt. 'What does he mean by that?'

'I don't know. He drinks on duty, just so you know.'

'Listen; I got to thinking that things started happening here, with the previous minister getting run down and killed. I could see if it was an accident.'

'Are you saying it wasn't an accident?'

'I'm saying it was a hit and run. Nobody knows anything. Even if it was one of the locals who was drunk, somebody would know about it the next morning. Then the new minister comes in. I wondered who else was new in town. Who was essentially a stranger coming into the compound as it were. Steffi and I got some info faxed through from Edinburgh before the lines went down and we were looking at it in my room.'

'What did you find out?' Watt asked.

'Although there are a lot of strangers in town with the play being put on tomorrow, there is one person in town who has only been here a short time, somebody who lives here now but has only been here a couple of months.'

'Who's that?'

'Eve Ross.'

'It doesn't mean to say she's had anything to do with the murders.'

'I'm not saying that for sure, but we should take another look at her.'

'I didn't know we'd had a look at her in the first place!' Watt said. 'Eve Ross? I can't see her having anything to do with it.'

Gibb stubbed out his cigarette. 'You've been spending time with her. Did she tell you anything about herself?'

'Not a lot. I mean, I didn't tie her to a fucking chair and interrogate her, if that's what you mean.'

'Calm down, son,' Gibb said. 'Let's just take it easy. And if you are giving her one, don't fall asleep on her for God's sake.'

'Jesus, Paddy. She's a sweet woman. We have a laugh.'

'Did she tell you her husband died in mysterious circumstances?' Miller said.

Watt looked at him, unsure what to say next.

'You didn't know she was married before, did you?'

'She never mentioned that. Christ, I only met her yesterday.'

'You're a fast worker, that's for sure.' Gibb said.

'We're just messing about. I mean, it's not as if I'm going to marry her.'

'What about Jean back home? She won't be pleased to find out you've been playing away from home.'

'It's just a bit of fun. I think Jean's been playing away too, so I don't see why she should get all the fun.'

'For God's sake. Revenge shagging. What next?'

'Do you know anything about her at all, Andy?' Miller said.

'I know she likes Pink Floyd.'

'Did you know she was originally from here in Langholm?'

Watt hesitated. 'No, I don't think she mentioned that.'

'She knows this place like the back of her hand.'

'Doesn't mean to say she's a nutter.'

'We're trying to establish who could be responsible. But you were with her at the boarding house, weren't you, Andy?' Miller said. 'She was with us at the bar, and then she was with you. That's a good enough alibi. Was she with you until we got the knock from Nick Jones?'

Watt looked at the two senior detectives. 'Fuck. No. She said she had to go tend to a patient. She left.'

'Where is she now?' Miller said.

'She got called away to the accident down by the bridge,' Watt answered.

'Go and pick her up,' Gibb said. 'Tell her she's needed back here. I want to have a word with her.'

'And accuse her of being a murderer?'

'No. I just want to talk to her.'

Miller and Watt left the station.

Nick Jones walked along High Street and across the Thomas Telford bridge. Who would have thought? Murders in Langholm? It was unthinkable, but good footing for working in Edinburgh.

The wind exploded across the bridge, blowing the snow hard. It blinded him as he made his way down the other side. He turned right into Frances Street and continued round into Mary Street.

That was a turn up for the books, Pinky Malone being a perv. Imagine calling a young lassie like Mary and threatening her over the phone. Christ, he had talked to Mary in a bar one night a couple of months ago, and he knew right away that she was trouble. What did Malone think he was doing? Nick knew that Mary would have given him what he wanted without scaring her. He himself had spent the night with her, and after that, he knew why she had never married; she was fucking mental.

Jesse's house was the first one. Opposite was a little grass area, now covered in several feet of snow, with the river beyond it. This was a nice street in the summer, but now it was just like what he imagined living in Siberia was all about.

He took out the key and opened the door. It was a relief being out of the snow. He tried a light switch, but no lights came on. He stamped his boots on the doormat and walked into the kitchen, taking a torch out of his pocket. The phone was in a drawer, he had been told. He opened each one, but couldn't find it. Was Malone lying? Maybe he had been mistaken and it was in the living room.

He walked through and stopped.

There was a man standing in the middle of the room wearing a ski mask. Nick grabbed his extendable baton. 'I'm a police officer,' he said. 'Keep your hands where I can see them.'

'That won't be necessary, officer. Just take it easy and you won't get hurt.'

'You take it fucking easy, and *you* won't get hurt. Or else you'll be eating this fucking baton.' He shone the light into the man's eyes but he couldn't tell who it was.

'Get on your fucking knees.'

'I don't think so.'

That's when Nick felt the metal gun barrel touch the back of his neck.

'Drop the baton, son. We really don't want to hurt you. But we will.'

For the first time since becoming a police officer, Nick Jones felt real fear.

THIRTY-THREE

Dan Brown woke up with his mouth feeling like he'd licked wallpaper paste. Where the hell was he? His head hurt and he didn't know where he was.

Had he been out with the rugby club boys again? *Fucked if I know.* If he had been, it had been one hell of a bender.

He tried to move his arms but they didn't seem to be working. He was lying on a bed in a small room. It was warm and comfortable but it wasn't his own room. Where the hell was it?

His eyes were a bit foggy. He couldn't focus them properly. He tried sitting up and that's when he realised that his hands were handcuffed together. Fuck. Had he been at a stag do or something? No, that wasn't it. Something was buzzing about on the edge of his periphery. He couldn't grasp it.

He sat up and blinding pain shot through his head. He got up off the bed and walked over to the door. Turned round and grabbed the door handle. The door was locked. Then he looked down. He wore a shirt but he wasn't wearing any trousers. Only underpants and socks.

Aw fuck. Where the hell was he? He listened at the door. No sound was coming from the other side. He padded over to the window. All he saw outside was snow on the ground and the trees that were only yards away. Snow was falling from the dark sky.

He went over to the bed and sat down. He felt like shaking his head to see if he could try and clear it, but he thought he might just have to sit here for a little while longer and think some more.

'Please tell me you don't think the doctor is a killer?' Watt said as Miller drove the Land Rover down the A7.

'I'm not saying that, Andy. But there's something not right about her. It's a feeling I have. Nobody seems to know anything about her, she lives in a boarding house. She's a loaner.'

'For God's sake, Frank. That doesn't make her a killer.'

'I know that, but right now, we have no suspects. And it's not like I'm going to come right out and ask her. She could be our killer though, Andy. She was friends with Ella and Ann. What if she was jealous of their relationship? We've both met people who have killed for less.'

'Christ almighty. I slept with her, Frank. Just thinking about it doesn't do much for my libido. And she was going to come back to my room when she had been out seeing her patient. Or murdering Mary Patterson, if we believe your story.'

Miller slowed down at Skipper's Bridge, the headlight beams bouncing off the snow that was banked up on either side of the bridge walls. On the other side were the blue flashing lights of an ambulance, a police car, and the Langholm fire engine.

Miller pulled in behind the vehicles and he and Watt got out into the snow.

'What happened?' he asked the fire commander.

'A car went down into the stream below. God knows who ordered the road dug up in this weather, but they made the bridge collapse. We're trying to get the driver out, but the weather is hindering us.'

'Have you seen the doctor?'

'She was here a little while ago, but she left when the ambulance crew turned up. The driver is okay, just shaken up and he'll have cuts and bruises, but he's not badly injured. He just got a fright.'

'Okay, thanks.' Miller turned to Watt. 'I wonder where the hell she went?'

'Christ, she was keen to get back to the boarding house. I'm going to tell her to bog off.'

They got back in the Land Rover and Miller was about to turn at the foot of Cemetery Road when something caught his eye. He kept the engine running but got back out to speak to the commander.

'Who lives up by the cemetery?'

'Nobody. It was a caretaker's house, but, you know, cutbacks and all that. Unless it was rented out. I don't know.'

Miller nodded and walked away, getting back into the car. 'He says nobody lives there, but look; there's smoke up there, like it's coming out of a chimney.'

'Let's go and have a look then. I'm in the mood for giving somebody a bloody good belting.'

Miller drove the car up the winding road until it opened up into a clearing at the top. The cemetery was ahead of them with the caretaker's cottage over on the left. He pulled in at the front gate. There were fresh tyre tracks here but they were starting to fill with snow indicating they hadn't been made at this minute, but somebody had indeed been here recently.

The two detectives got out and the wind was worse

up here, creating a blizzard. They walked up to the front door. Miller tried the handle.

'It's locked,' he shouted above the wind.

'I thought they all kept their fucking doors open!'

Miller felt a rush of frustration shoot through him and kicked the door at the lock. It exploded inwards. A flurry of snow blew in as they stepped inside.

Watt closed the door as best he could and they walked through the cottage, coming to a room at the back. That door too was locked.

Watt booted it and this door too flew open.

Sergeant Dan Brown was sitting on the bed.

'You Edinburgh wankers aren't too bad after all,' he said.

THIRTY-FOUR

Bloody typical Eve Ross thought. The windscreen wipers battled with the snow as she drove back up the A7. She wanted to spend another night with Andy. Her new boyfriend. But that fucker was going around killing people. She almost wished he would come to her so she could deal with him. Bastard.

Losing her friend was horrendous of course, but she didn't feel sad. As a doctor, she was used to seeing dead people all the time. But she couldn't focus on that. She had to focus on Andy. The new love of her life. Christ, she couldn't stop thinking about him. She could hear his voice, still feel the smoothness of his skin. His laughter was infectious. God, he was so good to be around.

You're into him in a big way, aren't you? Angel said from the back.

'I am. I'm head over heels, Angel.'

'I can't blame you. He's a keeper.'

The big Land Rover slipped sideways and she corrected it like an expert. She had thought this maybe wasn't a good idea coming here, but Simon had insisted. It was the last chance saloon, but what would he say when she told him that she had met somebody new? Surely he would be happy for her? Like Angel was.

She hoped so. If not, well, there were going to be many bridges to cross before she got to where she wanted to be.

At last, the town hall came into view. She had begun to hate the sight of the place until Andy had arrived. Now it was his place of work.

She felt bad for thinking her thoughts, but what if there were more murders? Andy would have to stay with the team. That would be superb. She laughed in the darkness of the car. A few people dying was neither here nor there, if her Andy would stay with her. And when the murders stopped, her very own detective would stay here in town with her.

She turned down by the hospital. This was a God-awful place. Nurses who couldn't tie their own fucking shoelaces without a PDF. A porter who thought he was all that and a poke of chips. With a nickname like some ponce. *Pinky*. George Malone thought he was God's gift, even though he had slightly protruding front teeth. He had the fucking cheek to smile at her one day. Yes, he was one of a small rota of staff, unlike Dumfries, and they would bump into each other a lot, but he gave her the creeps.

Luckily, he didn't know what she was really like. She laughed out loud.

She'd promised Simon she would be on her best behaviour and take her meds. She hadn't taken them yesterday and she hadn't taken them today.

That's my girl! Those fucking pills were keeping me away. You should have listened to me, not that fucking Simon.

'He's not that bad.'

Compared to what? Angel lit up a cigarette and blew the smoke into the car. She was about to chastise Angel about smoking in here, but then again, it wasn't real. Angel wasn't real. She was Eve's friend though, the one who was always with her, through all the bad times, and all the good times.

'Do you like Andy?' Eve asked out loud.

Angel laughed hard, the cigarette bobbing up and down on her lips. *Yeah. I like him a lot.*

'Thank God for that.'

You need my approval, sweets?

'I *want* your approval. I would *like* your approval.'

Just relax there. I like your new man. He's a

charmer, that's for sure. And good looking! Boy oh boy, if I was real, I'd want him to do me as well.

Eve beamed a smile at her. 'I am so glad you're back. I missed you a lot.'

Well, just don't take the little pills again. You don't need them anyway, do you?

'Of course not.'

As long as you don't take them, I'll be around. We can have fun again.

'Simon will be so mad. Nobody knows about me except him. If it wasn't for him, I wouldn't be a doctor anymore.'

Don't tell him then.

'Do you think I can get away with it?'

Of course you can. I'll help you.

Eve parked the car in the hospital car park. She got out, the snow driving down hard, and huddled as she walked along David Street, heading for the boarding house.

You meeting up with Andy tonight? Angel was walking beside her now and she slipped her arm through Eve's.

It felt good to have Angel right next to her again.

'Of course I am.' Eve smiled as they rounded the corner into John Street. A man was blocking her way. She stepped into the road to go round him, but he took a step sideways.

'Hello, Eve,' the man said.

She looked at him but he had a hood up with a scarf covering his lower face.

She didn't see the punch coming.

As she lay on the snow-covered road, she saw Angel standing screaming at the man, but he couldn't hear her.

Only Eve could hear her.

Then she couldn't hear anything.

THIRTY-FIVE

'Well, Sergeant Brown, maybe I should just kick you in the nuts now for calling us wankers,' Miller said. 'But seeing you standing there in your skids, I feel sorry for you.'

Watt just shook his head. 'Turn around.' He unlocked the cuffs and took them off Brown.

'Tell us why you're in here,' Miller said.

'Do you see my trousers anywhere around here?'

Miller switched a lamp on. They all looked around and Miller spotted the large man's trousers lying on the back of a chair.

'There they are, Andy.'

'I'm not touching them. Get them yourself, Brown.'

Brown staggered across in the dark and got his trousers and put them on.

'You been drinking?' Miller said.

'Yeah, that's what happened. I got pished and handcuffed myself after taking my trousers off.'

'Some blokes are kinky that way,' Watt said. 'Maybe you were leading up to putting your belt round your neck and hanging from the lavvy door handle next.'

'Put the kettle on and I'll tell you my theory of what I think's going on,' said Brown.

Watt went into the kitchen and put it on. 'I thought this place was supposed to be empty?' he said when he came back a few minutes later with the mugs of coffee.

'So did I. It seems it isn't.'

They sat down on the sofa. 'Tell us what's going on,' Miller said.

'I'll tell you why I came here, but first, let me tell you my theory. I was born and brought up here in Langholm. Lived here my whole life. Joined Lothian and Borders police when I was eighteen. I became a sergeant and was happy with my life. My work life. My personal life has gone to shit but never mind that. But you hear things about the town when you've lived here all your life. I heard the stories my father used to tell. He told me all about Hugh Abernethy, the young lad who was a brilliant writer, but who got called up to fight for his country during the second world war.' He drank some coffee.

'We've heard stories about Hugh,' Miller said.

'Maybe not this part. You see, we all know that Rudolph Hess flew to Scotland, supposedly to broker a peace deal with the UK. Long story short, he was trying to get to Dungavel Castle in Lanarkshire. The plane ran out of fuel, and he parachuted out and the plane crashed. What people don't know, and this is just rumour, but the plane Hess was flying landed here in Langholm. May 10, 1941. A farmer was in his house sleeping when he heard a plane coming in low. He thought it was going to crash, but it landed. Right up here. Before this was the new cemetery, it was a flat field. Long enough for a plane to land. The plane was met by none other than Hugh Abernethy himself. Documents were given to Hugh, then Hess took off again. We know that Hess crashed shortly afterwards. And then Hugh was sent overseas, to Iceland. From what I heard, he was flown to meet up with an American airman, who was supposed to fly back to the States, and Hugh was supposed to fly home here. But what happened after that, we don't know. The plane flew off course, then crashed on a glacier in Iceland.'

'What were the documents?' Watt asked. The logs in the fire crackled in the silence.

'Nobody knows. Hugh worked for Special Operations Executive.'

'And all of this is just hearsay?' Miller said.

'I heard the story from Ella Fitzroy years ago. She

had a box with gold coins in it. She said it was handed down to her and her sister. Supposedly, it was given to Hugh by Hess, along with some other boxes of gold. It was meant to be a goodwill gesture. Hess gave Hugh some documents detailing where a vast treasure trove was hidden. In Scotland.

'Hugh allegedly took the boxes of gold he was given and he hid them. He kept the small box of coins to show as proof, and he gave them to his father. But his father died shortly afterwards and Hugh went missing. Ella Fitzroy and Ann Fraser are Hugh's nieces. They fell heir to the coins. They didn't know the significance of them, for one reason or another.'

'And now you think that somebody thinks – or thought – that the women knew where the boxes of gold were hidden?'

'I do. I didn't connect it at first, but it all has to do with the war memorial they're erecting, with Hugh's name being added. It seems to have stirred something up and somebody now knows that there may be boxes of gold hidden somewhere in town.'

'There's gold in them thar hills,' Watt said.

'Somebody might be desperate enough to try and get that information. Maybe Ella wouldn't give it up and paid with her life.'

'Or she didn't know the answer and the killer didn't believe her,' Miller said. 'Ann's missing now, too.'

'Killers. There's more than one.'

They drank the coffee.

'Where do you come into this?' Miller asked. 'You were going to tell us how you came to be here.'

'I was suspicious about PC Nick Jones. I went to his house. I thought about going knocking on his door and having it out with him. I'd had a couple of wee nips and I was in the mood for boxing.'

'Where is he staying?'

'On Drover Road. Under his apartment is an old garage. A Land Rover came out while I was waiting, and I was curious as to where he was going. I followed the car here. When I came in, they were waiting. They knew who I was.'

'Did you get a good look at them?'

Brown shook his head. 'No. They were wearing balaclavas. One of them injected something into me. I woke up a little while ago.'

'Let's hope they come back soon,' Watt said.

'No, you don't want that, Watt. These guys are heavily armed and they know what they're doing.'

'We should leave. Get you checked out by the doctor,' Miller said.

'I just need to pee first,' Brown said, getting up slowly and going through to look for a bathroom.

'Do you still think Eve Ross had anything to do with this?' Watt said.

'To be honest, I didn't really think she had in the first place. I just wanted to make sure, but now I don't think she had anything to do with the murders. We need to find her to get her to check Brown out.'

Miller got up and went looking through the house. It was certainly being lived in as he found clothes in the bedroom. Male clothes. Nothing of a personal nature, nothing with a person's name on it. But Miller did find one item of clothing that took his breath away for a second.

He went back to the living room just as Brown came back. 'We need to leave. Now. Whoever is living here will be back soon.'

'I want to take my car if it's still outside.'

'I think you should ride with us, Dan,' Miller said.

When they got back out, the snow had eased off. Brown couldn't see his car around. 'Shite. They must have done something to my car. I don't seem to have a choice in the matter now.'

They got into the Land Rover and Miller drove carefully down the hill.

They made it back to town and stopped at the hospital. They were told that Eve's Land Rover was in the car park so she must be at home. They drove along and parked round from the boarding house.

When they went in, Watt went up to her door and knocked. There was no answer. They woke up Bunty and had her open the door. The room was empty, so Miller asked her if there was anywhere Sergeant Brown could sleep for the night as they had to get something sorted out and he couldn't go back home tonight.

'You can sleep on my couch, Sergeant Brown. My husband snores like a pig, but I'm sure you can sleep right through it.'

Miller and Watt went back upstairs. 'We can't go searching for Eve right now, and the guys who overpowered Brown will look at the hospital for him, or his house. We might as well get some sleep.'

'Agreed.' They went their separate ways, and when Watt got into his room, he jammed a chair under the door handle.

THIRTY-SIX

Steffi went back to the boarding house to look for Miller. She couldn't find any of them, so she looked through the papers again. Thank God they had downloaded things before the phones went out.

There was something bugging her. She felt dog tired and it was after midnight now but sleep wouldn't come even if she lay down.

She wondered if Miller had been reading through his copies. Of course, they'd gone through them together but they each had their own copy. She had to admit that she was stubborn. When she got her teeth into something, she wouldn't let go. And something about this was bothering her. Not the murders, but something she'd read in all the printouts.

She started rifling through them again. Started reading through the reports they'd got in on each of the people they'd requested information on. Then she stopped at one in particular.

She thought she knew who the next victim was going to be. Normally, getting on her mobile phone or the Airwave would be the answer for getting back-up, but neither thing was an option. Should she wait for help? No. She hadn't acted like that in the army, and she sure as hell wouldn't be doing that now. Somebody's life was in danger.

It wasn't that far from here. She could walk, even although the snow was thick, she could still make good time.

Steffi left her room quietly and walked down the stairs, trying not to wake Bunty. She left the boarding house, wondering if she should go along to the hotel and find Gibb, or at least Julie. She couldn't call of course, and she didn't want to waste time.

She started walking through the deep snow. Left, towards the Thomas Telford bridge. She walked past it, her boots kicking the snow out of the way. It hadn't stopped snowing, but it had eased off. She crossed the road at the corner and took the road that led off on the right, opposite the little visitors' centre. A sign attached to the lamppost pointed to the golf course and another said there was no footway for four hundred yards. She kept to the low wall on the left as she approached the blind corner. There wasn't much chance of any traffic coming round the bend, but she didn't want to take it for granted. There was a high wall on the right and there was no way to see anything if it came round here.

She walked under a canopy of snow-covered trees before the road opened up again. The road rounded to the left and at the top of the short hill, she came to the old gatehouse for the mansion. The gates were open and she could see tyre tracks in the deep snow.

She walked up the driveway, feeling herself sweating beneath her winter coat. At the top, the driveway veered to the right and then she saw the magnificent house itself, sitting in the middle of the grounds.

Snow covered everything. Except the Land Rover sitting in front of the door. It only had a light coating on it.

She walked up, her legs feeling tired now. There were no lights on in the house, but she saw the door was slightly ajar.

Jesus, what if the killer was already inside?

Come on, Steffi, you've been in worse situations than this overseas. Get a grip of yourself.

She knew she could fight, and no human being ever scared her.

She gently pushed the door. She couldn't hear anything but the wind rushing up the hills and through the extensive grounds. She walked inside and gently closed the front door behind her. This was a little vestibule. It sounded deathly quiet in the house now. She opened the door in front of her and stepped into a large hallway. It had a glass-domed cupola above the huge staircase. It was covered with snow but it wasn't as pitch dark as she thought it might be.

She could make out half a dozen doors leading off the hallway. Only the one on her right was open. She took a step towards it. The door wasn't fully open and there was no light on, but she pushed it gently open and walked in.

Now she knew where Graham Gorman had gone.

He was sitting in a chair in the middle of the room. Underneath was a large plastic sheet, where most of his entrails had landed. Blood had poured out of his mouth in the final throes of death.

Steffi could feel herself starting to freeze as fear kicked in but she forced herself to carry on. It was clear nobody else was in the room as the chair was the only furniture. She walked round until she was standing right in front of Gorman. It looked like he had been dead for some time.

Backing out as quietly as she could, she brought out a little flashlight to shine around the hallway, all thoughts of stealth now gone.

She saw the faintest hint of a light coming from under another door. She stepped forward and put her ear to the door. She could hear faint voices. Grabbing the door handle as gently as she could, she turned it and held onto it, slowly opening the door.

It was a home cinema with three rows of seats facing her.

A huge TV screen was on her right.

But it was the person sitting in one of the chairs in the front row that had her transfixed.

'Come in,' he said.

She hesitated. She could make out the figure of a woman sitting in the dark. The flickering lights from the TV showed her throat had been cut.

And that's when she felt the fingers grab her hair and put the knife to her throat.

Steffi Walker realised she had made the biggest mistake of her life.

THIRTY-SEVEN

'I don't know about you, boss, but I'm bloody knackered,' Andy Watt said to Miller.

'Were you up to your old tricks again?'

'Meaning what?'

'Entertaining the doctor.'

'I don't think so. I wish I hadn't entertained her at
all, now.'

Dan Brown was in the living room watching breakfast TV.

'You might want to keep a low profile,' Miller said
to him. 'They'll be looking for you.'

'I'll hang out here, but if you need me for anything,
just holler.'

Miller and Watt went to stand in the lobby. 'Did
you knock on Steffi's door?'

'I did but she didn't answer.'

Bunty came walking in from her own quarters. 'Do you need anything?' She spoke as if she was suspicious of them.

'We need you to open our colleague's door and see she's alright.'

They followed her up the stairs to Steffi's room. 'We'll stay back a bit in case she's not decent,' Miller said. Bunty knocked, got no answer so let herself in.

'It's empty. The bed hasn't been slept in.'

Miller looked for himself. He saw the sheets of paper lying on the bed and had a look at them. 'Thank you,' he said to Bunty after gathering the papers up.

'What about Eve Ross?' Knock on her door, Andy.'

'I already did. No reply.'

Bunty got the key for her room and found it empty.

Downstairs, Miller spoke to Watt again. 'These are the documents we had faxed through. We were looking at who were basically strangers.'

'Not many I'm sure.'

'I want to go and get Gibb. I won't say anything yet, but I want him to come with us to talk to somebody.'

They went out into the murky daytime. The snow was coming down yet again. They stepped out as fast as they could along to the hotel. Gibb was sitting with Julie, eating breakfast.

'Pull up a pew,' he said, washing his sausage down with some coffee.

'The breakfast is good,' Julie said.

'We don't have time for breakfast. Let me you ask you, sir; what did Nick Jones find at Jesse's house last night?'

'Nobody came back. Jones or the doctor.'

Miller sat at the table and told Gibb about Dan Brown. 'I might be wrong here, but we need to go and speak to somebody.'

'Who?' Gibb said.

'Somebody who isn't all he seems to be.'

They left Julie to go and check on Nick Jones at the house he rented, the one Brown had told them about.

Miller drove the Land Rover into the churchyard. There were another two Landies in there.

'Christ, I bet Land Rover make a fortune from country folks,' Watt said, getting out of their own car. Miller parked it so that it blocked the exit from the church, at the bridge.

They went to the church door and walked in quietly. Then down to Michael Monro's office door.

Miller opened it without knocking.

'I thought I'd find you here,' he said to the two men. Michael Monro and Sergeant Hudson.

Monro smiled and Hudson took a step towards the

two detectives. Watt brought his extendable baton out and flexed it open.

'That's right, sergeant. You bring it on if you think you're hard enough, and I'll bury this fucking baton right in your fucking skull.'

Hudson hesitated and looked at Monro. Now Miller knew who was in charge.

'It was you two who drugged Sergeant Brown, wasn't it?' Miller said.

Monro smiled even wider. 'Now don't go doing anything stupid, Inspector Miller. And to answer your question, yes, it was. We didn't want to harm him, we just wanted him out of the way for a bit.' He stepped round his desk and Miller took a step towards him, feeling the adrenaline shoot into him.

Monro held up his hands. 'Nobody's going to do anything rash.' He looked at Hudson. 'And I mean nobody. Besides, I just want to talk.'

'You'll get the chance to talk up at the station. You're coming with us.'

'I can't do that, Frank.'

'You don't have a choice,' Watt said.

'I do, sergeant. If you'll kindly look behind you.'

He and Miller both looked round at a man dressed in white camouflage, pointing a silenced gun at them, another man dressed similarly standing right behind him.

'Come on, let's go through to the committee room and we can all have a nice cuppa. Hudson, get the kettle on.'

Miller and Watt walked through with the gunmen standing far enough back so they couldn't be jumped, but close enough so that they wouldn't miss should they have to open fire.

In the committee room where the Hugh Abernethy memorial paraphernalia was laid out, Miller and Watt sat down at the table while Hudson bustled about with the tea. Monro sat at the head of the table.

'You killed all those people,' Miller said as Hudson put the tea down.

'Deary me, of course not. Yes, my two men did destroy the communications tower. They also took out the bridges. It's what we do, Frank. We were sent here to find something, and we are still looking.'

'You're trying to tell me you didn't murder Ella and young Mary, and take Ann? And what about Graham Gorman?'

'I'm telling you the truth, Frank. We did not kill anybody. If we had, I would have my men put a bullet in your brain right now and take you somewhere, and I can promise you, nobody would ever find your body. But that's not how we work.'

Ken Smart and Eddie Hooper nodded. 'We're experts at blowing things up, but we don't go around killing old women and young girls.' It was Hooper who spoke. *He even sounds hard,* Miller thought.

'You see, we work for the government,' Monro said.

'Let me guess; when Hugh Abernethy was discovered in the ice, that rang alarm bells. So you and your cronies were sent here to try and find the gold. We know all about Rudolph Hess landing here and meeting with Abernethy.'

'I thought you might find out about that meeting. But there is no gold. That was a myth. The little box of gold that Hess gave to Hugh was a token.'

'Then what are you looking for?'

'That's classified,' Hudson said.

'We can't tell you exactly what we were looking for,' Monro said, 'but it's not gold. Just documents. When Hugh was found, we thought he would have certain documents in his briefcase. He didn't. We thought he might have left them here.'

Neither detective drank their tea. 'If you didn't kill those people, then who did? And where's Gorman?'

Monro leaned forward and took a sip out of each cup, on the opposite side. 'There's nothing in the tea, I promise you. As I said, if we wanted rid of you, we could just shoot you.'

Watt shrugged and drank some.

'To answer your question, I don't know who killed those people. It was very disconcerting.'

'Are you working with Nick Jones?' Miller asked.

'That young PC? No, he's not one of ours.'

'Dan Brown said he saw a car coming out of the garage underneath the apartment Jones rents.'

'Yes, indeed. Jones rents the apartment, Hudson rents the garage.'

Miller nodded. 'Brown saw Hudson coming out of the garage and thought it was Jones.'

'He did indeed. That's how we caught him up at the caretaker's cottage.'

'Now what? You just shoot us and make us disappear?' Watt said, trying to stay casual, but shaking inside.

'I told you, you don't have to worry. We're finished here. We searched Ella and Ann's house and found nothing. We're moving out.'

'What about the previous minister? Did you kill him?' Miller said.

'No, we didn't. Our plan was to have him take early retirement. We would have taken him away on holiday first. He was an old man. We don't kill old people. He genuinely was killed by a hit-and-run driver. He did like a little whisky or two. Who knows what happened, Frank? It wasn't up to us though. I was coming here whether he was here or not.'

'What about the truck driver? The one who was driving the tanker that crashed into the bridge?'

'Yes, we orchestrated that. But he's safe. My colleagues were acting as security guards at the old police station. He's been kept against his will, in the cells below the station, but he hasn't been ill-treated. He's warm, has food, and we even put a TV in his cell, so he wouldn't get bored. He also has company; a local man who came upon my men when they were putting boulders down on the road to block it. They had to knock him out, but they're trained paramedics. He's got a sore head, but he'll be fine. His car will be replaced by a brand new one. The tanker too will be replaced. Oh, and we had Jesse Gorman's house bugged. We'd gone to take the bugs out when young Nick came into the house, looking for the throwaway phone. He's in the jail cells too.'

'This has been an expensive search.'

'No cost is ever too much when it comes to national security. Don't worry, the men will be dropped off at the police station when we leave. The real one at the town hall.'

'You're just leaving?' Watt said. 'Just like that?'

'Our job here is done. We've been here a couple of months. Time for us to go.'

'It's a bit of a coincidence that you guys appear and people involved with the committee start to die. I don't believe in coincidences,' Miller said.

'Neither do I, Frank,' Monro said. 'That's why

somebody else came here, looking for gold that didn't exist, but they didn't know that. They killed those people, trying to find the location. Whoever it is, it isn't any of us.'

'How are you going to get out?'

'We have satellite radios. The clean-up crews are already on their way in. Our boss in London has roped in the Royal Engineers. The bridges and roads that we destroyed will be fixed in a day. There's a communications team with them. They'll have the tower rebuilt and put back together in a day. The boulders will be removed. There's a very large team moving into Langholm as we speak. Everything will be exactly like it was before. They'll stay and help keep the roads clear.'

'The town's going to be short of a sergeant when you go, Hudson. Or whatever your name is.'

'Young Nick Jones will be good for this place. If he doesn't still want to go to Edinburgh, that is.'

Watt looked at Miller before looking at Monro. 'What now?'

Monro smiled. 'You're free to go. You'll never see us again.'

The two detectives got up and Miller was about to walk through the doorway behind Miller when Monro stopped him.

'Say hello to Neil McGovern when you get home, Frank.'

'He knows McGovern?' Watt said.

'Apparently. It's also a thinly veiled threat. He knows everything about me.'

Monro smiled again. 'There's no threat. I just had you all checked out when you arrived in town. In fact, I spoke to Neil on the phone. He told me to look out for you. I told him if there was anything you needed...'

'In that case.' Miller walked back to the table. 'If I'm right, then one of my officers is in trouble. I need your help.'

Monro looked at the sheet of paper Miller had put down in front of him. 'You came to the right man.' He looked at Smart and Hooper. 'One more job to do before we go home boys.'

THIRTY-EIGHT

'You fucking bitch! Tell me what you know!' the man screamed at her again.

Steffi Walker was stiff from being tied to the chair. She'd been here for hours. Her neck was stiff, her arms were sore from her hands being tied behind her back.

'I don't know anything. I swear.'

He slapped her again. Hard. Her cheek buzzed with the sting of his hand across her face. He grabbed her hair and pulled her face close to his. She could smell his foetid breath. His eyes were bloodshot but they were wide, as if only insanity lived behind them.

'Tell me where the fucking gold is!' He shouted inches from her face.

Gold? What the fuck was he talking about? 'I don't know anything about gold. I swear'

He roared, let her hair go and stepped back and

slapped her hard again, this time knocking her sideways. She landed on the fresh sheet of polythene he'd obviously put down in preparation for bringing her in here.

She caught sight of him leaping over towards her and she thought he was going to kick her in the face but he grabbed the chair and lifted her up with ease. He had enormous strength, probably fuelled by adrenaline.

'I'm going to ask you one more time and then I'm going to start cutting you.'

'Please don't. I would tell you. I have no reason not to.'

Then the blade appeared out of nowhere, like he was a magician. 'I'll start by cutting your ears off. Then your nose and then your lady bits.' He ran the knife gently over her breasts through her shirt. She just realised that he had taken her jacket off at some point.

The door opened and the woman appeared. 'I'm going out for a smoke,' she said simply. It wasn't a request, just an FYI. Then the door was closed again.

He looked at Steffi and smiled. 'Just you and me now. Which body part do you want to lose first?'

He lifted the large kitchen knife in front of her face.

'Wait!' she said. 'I think I might know where it is.'

'You're lying.'

'I'm not. I just remembered.'

'So tell me.'

The air was so bitterly cold. The wind whipped her cigarette smoke away. She stood huddled inside the overly large jacket, trying to stay warm. She wanted away from this God-awful place. There was nothing here. What did people do for fun?

She heard a scream coming from inside and laughed. He was having fun with her. Maybe if more people had that kind of fun, life round here would be more exciting.

She liked this house. Pity they couldn't keep it. Nine bedrooms it had. They could have their friends round for some wild parties.

She was about to go back in the house when she thought she saw movement. On the front lawn. She took a step forward and then she thought she was seeing things. Snow was rising up in one fluid movement, and before she had a chance to shout or move, two things moved towards her.

The things had eyes and they were both on top of her before she knew what was happening. Eddie Hooper grabbed the woman by the head and spun her round, putting a hand over her mouth. He brought a knife round, pulling her close to the door.

The other one had a silenced rifle pointing at her head.

'I'm going to take my hand off your mouth, but if I even think you're going to shout, I'll slit your fucking throat before you can even get a breath out. Understand?'

She nodded. The tip of the knife was already under her skin and she could feel the warm trickle of blood running down her throat.

'Where is he?' the man asked her quietly.

Ken Smart put the rifle inches from her left eyeball. 'The bullet will cut right through your fucking brain stem if you shout,' he warned.

'In the living room.' She spoke so softly; her words were taken away by the wind.

'What?' Hooper said.

'The living room. Through the front door. First door on your right. He's got her in there. He's going to kill her.'

Hooper lifted an arm, his fist bunched. Two more men in white camouflage appeared from round the end of the building where they'd been watching. One of them pulled out handcuffs and got her hands behind her back.

'Is he armed?' Miller asked her.

'Yes. He has a big knife. He's mental and he's going to kill her if he hasn't already.'

Watt put a gloved hand round the woman's mouth and pulled her backwards. Julie, dressed like the others, helped him take her round the side of the house out of sight.

'I'm going in,' Miller said.

Eddie Hooper put a hand on his chest. 'We're used to doing this stuff, Frank. He won't even hear us coming.'

Miller could barely keep it together. 'She's more than just a member of my team; she's like family.'

'Okay. Stay behind us. Got it?' Miller now noticed that Hooper too had a rifle, slung over his shoulder, painted in the camouflage colours.

He nodded.

Hooper and Smart went in fast but quiet. Miller didn't think he'd ever heard people move so quietly.

They went up to the door of the living room where they heard shouting. Hooper had his rifle out. Miller heard the two words, just before the two men in front opened the door: *kill you!*

Eddie Hooper opened the door in one silent movement, saw the woman tied to the chair, saw the man look up in surprise.

Stuart Love knew it was over. He pulled his arm back, about to bring the knife back down, but before it could even begin its return journey, Hooper lifted his rifle and fired in one smooth action. Ken Smart, just a little off to one side, fired at almost the same time.

Stuart Love was thrown back off his feet, his knife not even coming near Steffi again. The back of his head exploded over the carpet.

Miller pushed past and ran over to Steffi, putting his arms around her head. 'God, Steffi, I thought you were a goner.'

'I'm fine. He's working with Nancy Corbett, his girlfriend.'

'I know. We got her.'

'Dr Ross is here too. We were in the same room for a while, but then we were separated.'

Hooper and Smart stood over Love's body and shot him in the heart. Just to make sure. Miller and Steffi winced. Miller supposed that's what they were trained to do in special forces.

Watt and Julie appeared. 'Uniforms have the female,' he said.

'Eve Ross must be in here somewhere,' Miller told Watt, just as more uniforms rushed in.

'Get searching for the doctor!'

They found her a few minutes later, next door in the home cinema. Sitting next to the cold corpse of Ann Fraser. Eve Ross was fine.

'Don't you do that to me again,' Miller said to Steffi as he cut the cable ties.

Steffi threw her arms around him. 'I'm ready to go home, sir.'

'Me too.'

THIRTY-NINE

Dan Brown was back in uniform by the afternoon. So was Nick Jones. 'Son, you want my opinion, you stay as acting sergeant here until they can take you in Edinburgh. There's nothing here for a young laddie like you. I was just being an arse.'

'Thank you, sir.'

'No more *sir*. We're both sergeants. You stepped up when it counted. And we both got taken by those guys but after what I was told they could do, I won't argue with them.'

Gibb came into the room with the other detectives. 'Dr Ross is fine. They just tied her up, but they didn't get round to hurting her. She's looking after Steffi just now. Steffi will be fine. Just a few bruises.'

They sat down at the table.

'Nancy Corbett will be taken down to Dumfries to

be processed there,' Miller said. 'The army engineers have already sorted a temporary fix to the road south of Skipper's Bridge. They're clearing the roads with ploughs and tractors and all sorts of machinery. It won't be long before they're right through the town and they're staying here until this storm passes.'

'What about the bridge on the north side of town?' Watt said.

'They're going to be working on it as soon as they get through town.'

'Where are Monro and Hudson now? And the two other men?'

'Like ghosts,' Miller said, 'we saw them one minute, and then they were gone.'

Julie drank some coffee. 'Nancy keeps maintaining it was Stuart Love who did the murders. She says she was terrified of him. Love was broke, and it was his idea to put on this play in town so he could come here to look for what he thought were boxes of gold hidden somewhere. He'd heard the stories when he was a wee boy growing up here. He was convinced his aunts knew the location.'

'I hope she has enough money to hire the best lawyers,' Gibb said.

'This was all about money?' Nick asked.

'Some people are desperate, son,' Gibb said.

'Why did Steffi go up to the house?'

'She said that she was reading information we'd requested about people who were new in town,' Miller said. 'She couldn't understand why Stuart Love was renting that mansion when the information came back on him revealing he was broke. She thought maybe he was getting a good deal because of who he was, but she also thought he was in trouble.'

'And she ended up walking in on the serial killer.'

'Exactly.'

There was a knock on the door. Eve Ross. 'Can I talk with you, Andy?'

Watt got up out of his chair and went out into the corridor with her. 'Everything okay? Well, you know what I mean. I know what you've just been through is horrific—'

'That's not what I want to talk to you about, Andy,' Eve said, interrupting him.

'Okay. I'm listening.'

Eve seemed unsure of herself for a moment. 'When I was sitting in that stupid home cinema, I had time to think. I kept saying to myself, if I get out of this, I want to do something more with my life. Being with you made me realise there are more things out there. I just wanted to say thank you for being with me.'

He smiled at her. 'We had some good fun in the short time we knew each other,' he said.

'I know. I've known some real arseholes in my life,

but you are completely different. You made me laugh, you made me smile. I was going through a really tough patch before I came here, but you made me see the light at the end of the tunnel.'

'This has certainly been some adventure.'

She reached up and kissed his cheek. 'I'm sure I'll see you again one day, Andy.' She turned and walked away as Watt went back into the incident room.

'What was all that about?' Miller said.

Watt looked at the door. 'Oh, we were just saying goodbye.' *I hope.*

As Eve Ross walked down the stairs, she turned to look at Angel. 'I think Andy Watt is going to like you.'

'I'm sure he is. If he could only see me, then he would be smitten.'

'He's smitten with me. Did you see the way he looked at me?'

'I did.'

'I can see great things in my future, Angel. Great things.'

FORTY

Three months later

There was nothing left of the old war memorial. The demolition crew had taken it down safely and all that remained was for the concrete base to be removed. One of the men positioned the jackhammer on the back of the JCB and let the machine do all the hard work. After an hour, the concrete base was gone.

The second one saw something sticking out of the dirt. 'Hey, what's this? A treasure chest.'

'What? Treasure? Don't talk pish.'

'It might be a box of gold.'

'Dream on.' He jumped out of the JCB into the breeze. The hot June air was making the JCB feel like an oven. 'Dig it up. What are you waiting for?'

His friend got a shovel and dug the dirt away from around it and then he lifted it out. An old lead box with a handle.

'Open it then.'

The man opened the box and looked inside. It contained nothing but an old notebook. He handed his friend the box and opened the book. 'There's a name in here. Hugh Abernethy. It looks like some play or something.'

'Let me see it.' He handed the box back and looked inside, flipping through the pages. 'What a load of crap. Some pish about Rudolph Hess. Just get rid of it.'

The first man took the box and the notebook and threw it into the skip next to where they were working. It was soon covered by pieces of the old war memorial.

AFTERWORD

This just leaves me to thank the people who come on each journey with me. My wife, Debbie, my daughters, Stephanie and Samantha.

Also, a big thank you to – in no particular order – Louise, Wendy, Julie, Fiona, Jeni, Michelle, Tracey, Evelyn, Merrill and Vanessa.

And last but not least, thanks to you, the reader, who make it all worthwhile.

If you enjoyed this book, please consider leaving a review. It makes all the difference to authors like me.

'Til next time!

John Carson
New York
September 2018

ABOUT THE AUTHOR

John Carson is originally from Edinburgh, Scotland, but now lives with his wife and family in New York State. And two dogs. And four cats.

www.johncarsonauthor.com

Printed in Great Britain
by Amazon